ALL FOR NAUGHT

ALL FOR NAUGHT

JOHN E. STITH

WILDSIDE PRESS

ALL FOR NAUGHT

CONTENTS

INTRODUCTION

"Naught for Hire" (*Analog*, July 1990, a novella) and "Naught Again" (*Analog*, November 1992, a novelette) are a bit of a departure from most of my other work, so I agreed to write a short introduction for the pair of stories.

For several years I had been keeping a file of the humorous ways technology was failing me. I labeled the file "Science doesn't work." I did nothing with the ideas for a long while, though, because that basic premise is contrary to my true feelings. While individual characters can often espouse values the author doesn't agree with, readers of my novels will probably draw the conclusion, correctly, that I feel science has the potential to allow the human race to survive. If we can establish pockets of humanity away from Earth before a global accident has the potential to wipe out our species, we have the potential to keep learning and growing in other environments.

One of my other concerns is the state of our educational system as it is attacked by agenda-driven groups fighting to teach their own religious doctrine to people of every religion by calling it "science" and completely missing the point of what science is. Typical readers of my work know that science embodies the process of continually questioning explanations and theories, and to label a doctrine that cannot be subjected to any scrutiny or questioning as a "science" is a step toward chaos. (Just for the record, I'm one of those people who happen to believe that science and religion can co-exist as long as they are understood to be different kinds of things.)

Anyway, by melding the failing-science ideas and the educational system concerns, I finally had a way of saying what I wanted to say, that a well-educated population can employ technology in fresh

and liberating ways, while the combination of poorly trained techni-
cians and poorly designed devices, gives us the potential to create an
enormously frustrating future. So the future of "Naught for Hire" is
yet another future-to-be-avoided, just as *1984* was not prediction but
a warning.

Of course any work of fiction that spends its time moralizing
isn't going to be very entertaining. My goal was to provide enough
entertainment that readers wind up laughing a lot, but when the
laughter stops, some of them may also start thinking about what
kind of future we want to build for ourselves.

When I sent the first story to Stan Schmidt at *Analog*, he called
to say that he was buying it, not because it is a typical *Analog* story —
it isn't — but he found it really funny. I've since had it reaffirmed
that humor is subjective; some will find things to laugh at and some
will not. I hope a few new readers will get some laughs this time
around.

— John E. Stith

NAUGHT FOR HIRE

LATE at night in a deserted Los Angeles office, a telephone rang once. The echoes died as a phone answerer sprang obediently to life.

The recorded voice spoke, baritone and slightly hoarse. "Nick Naught private investigations. I'm not all here right now, so please leave a message or a threat."

A soft voice came from the speaker. "Nick, this is Heather. I'm free next weekend, and I've got a neat new vid on massages. Call me if you're interested, okay?" A high-pitched *click* gave way to dial tone, then silence filled the Spartan office.

In the phone answerer, the *message waiting* circuit turned on. Then, softer than the faint air conditioning whine, a small voice said, "Nahhh."

The *message waiting* circuit turned off.

An attentive listener, who by this time of night would have been bored silly, could have heard an ever so faint laugh.

Chapter 1

IN a one-bedroom L.A. apartment, faint gray light, nearly exhausted from having traveled through thick smog, penetrated a window and illuminated a wall poster showing a South Seas island. The vivid blue water and the sparkling white beach, backdropped with an array of greens, would for some people have been almost enough to displace the sensations of thick air and gritty streets.

Next to the poster hung a framed quote. Lettered in the same mock-stitch style as folksy home-sweet-home signs, the words read, "Nostradufus: I have seen the future and it sucks."

The sound of a distant siren rose and fell like waves lapping against the shore, and the noise mingled with Nick Naught's relaxed breathing. A faint smile on his lips said he was dreaming he was on the island pictured near his bed, probably lying back in a comfortable beach chair and sifting the sparkling clean sand through his fingers.

From near Nick's bed came a soft *click*.

Ending the calm and untroubled atmosphere, the digital alarm clock began to play the only song it knew: reveille. Three surfaces of the alarm clock showed cracks from having fallen to the hard floor. Two segments of the display were out, so the eight looked like a three. The alarm droned on, its tone more like a kazoo than the bugle it had started life as.

Nick snorted and squeezed his already closed eyes even more tightly closed. For an instant, he wished he was some kind of mutant and could squeeze his ears closed.

He fumbled for the alarm. Almost immediately he knocked it onto the floor. The alarm bounced, and two final notes trailed off into silence, as if an arrow had taken the life of a very conscientious bugler.

Nick made a feeble attempt to rise. He imagined this was how it felt to be just coming out of open-heart surgery. He touched his chest, to see if he could feel any stitches or syntheskin. Nope.

After a deep breath, he hesitated, then grabbed for something beside the bed. His fingers made contact on the second try, and he pulled it up to his level.

A jumper cable.

Still mostly asleep, he bent forward and after a couple of tries managed to fasten the black cable to a band affixed around his ankle.

His fingers fumbled by the bed again and came up with a red jumper cable, which he fastened to a band around his wrist. His wrist flopped back onto the bed, and the cable swayed but kept its grip. The other end of the cable led to a large, heavy battery beside the bed. On the side of the battery was a colorful label saying, "Morning Jump Start."

Nick yawned and sighed. He fumbled again, near the head of the bed. His fingers found a large switch. He patted it the way a small child would pat a stuffed bear that had strayed too far from reach.

It was time. If he quit now, he'd be fast asleep in seconds. He summoned strength, and he flicked the switch that triggered a shrill electrical buzzing noise reminiscent of a failing neon sign. Nick was instantly galvanized. His eyes popped wide open, then promptly squeezed closed again. He screamed and writhed on the bed, like a snake with its tail caught in a mousetrap.

Barely able to muster a rational thought, he reached for the switch to turn the current off. Where was it? He fumbled for it. His fingers touched it! And he knocked it onto the floor. God, no, he must be wrong.

He groaned agonizingly, like a patient in electroshock. Still writhing under the pain and struggling madly, he reached for the floor and groped for the switch. Sweat stood out on his forehead. Where was that switch? This couldn't be happening. He searched to the left and searched to the right, and finally his fingers reached the switch housing. He maneuvered it so his fingers found the switch itself, and he finally managed to turn it off.

Instant silence. Nick fell back to the bed and resumed breathing. He rubbed his eyes and began to relax, feeling hardly more energetic than when he had first woke. After a long minute, he finally dragged himself into a sitting position, legs over the side of the bed and sighed. He blinked hard several times. Even the dim light seemed bright.

He said, to no one in particular, "Man, I hate Mondays."

Nick pulled the jumper cable off his ankle and let it drop to the floor. He pulled the cable off his wrist. He stared at the one from his wrist for a long second, then looked back at the switch. He moved the jumper cable toward his wrist and away again, and now that he could think clearly again, he realized he had not needed to look for the switch. He grimaced and got out of bed.

He managed to stub his toe on the way to the bathroom.

Squinting in the brighter light at the bathroom mirror, Nick sprayed a white foam into his hand. He spread it over his stubble, then rinsed his hands. He rested his hands on the sink until, moments later, he picked at the edge of the foam, which had turned hard, like a rubbery mask. With an abrupt, firm yank, he ripped the whole thing off his face, and he screamed. He inspected his smooth cheeks as he dropped the foam mask into the toilet and flushed. As the mask swirled in the water, it dissolved, leaving what was left of his stubble in the bubbling remains.

Nick was feeling a little more awake by the time the elevator reached his floor. *Bing.* The doors opened. As Nick entered the empty elevator, it said, "Good morning!" in a voice inhumanly cheerful for this time of day.

"Morning," Nick forced himself to say.

"What floor please?" The elevator's voice was copied from a nerdy, bow-tied comic actor of a decade past. Mixed in with the overdone cheerfulness was a nasal twang.

"One," Nick said softly.

"Thank you!" The elevator sounded as pleased as Pinocchio had been at becoming a real boy.

The door closed, and the elevator dropped two floors before it had to stop for another rider. The doors opened, and a frowning, burly guy got on with Nick. The man's coat sleeves were so short, his digital watch showed on the arm with the briefcase.

"Good morning!" said the cheerful elevator.

"Morning." The man's nod took in Nick. He turned around to face the door and assumed standard elevator posture, dutifully looking at the motionless floor indicator.

"What floor please?"

"Five," said the man. His voice seemed to be naturally loud thanks to the smooth walls all reflecting the sound so well.

The elevator hesitated. "What?"

The man spoke louder. "Five."

"What?" asked the elevator, using exactly the same intonation it had used the first time.

Nick grimaced. He tapped the man on the arm, about to say something, but the man ignored him.

"Five!" the man shouted.

Nick winced.

"What?"

Nick sighed and put a hand over his eyes. The high volume made his head hurt.

The man screamed, "Five!"

"What?"

The man's face colored. He sucked a full load of air into his chest and moved toward the microphone grill.

Nick whispered quickly, "Five." Experience had told him the elevator's voice-sensitivity setting was out of whack.

"Thank you!" said the elevator.

The man, still with lungs bloated with air, looked at Nick, amazed, as the elevator doors finally closed. The two men dropped in silence four more floors, and the elevator admitted a woman wearing a green business suit. In one hand, she held a book-viewer that seemed to absorb most of her attention.

"Good morning!" said the elevator.

Apparently absorbed in her reading, the woman ignored it. The elevator doors stayed open.

The elevator said, "I *said* good morning."

The woman suddenly looked up from her display, and her eyes opened wide in surprise. "Morning."

"What floor please?" the elevator asked, sounding much happier.

"Six."

The burly guy looked like he was hoping the elevator would give her a hard time, too, but the elevator merely said, "Thank you!"

The man looked disappointed as the elevator doors closed and the elevator started to drop.

It stopped at the sixth floor and the woman got off.

"Have a nice day!" said the elevator.

The elevator dropped to the fifth floor, where the burly guy scowled at the speaker grill and got off.

The elevator repeated its refrain. "Have a nice day!" As the doors began to close, the elevator voice added, more softly, "Dipstick."

The burly guy hesitated, still facing away from the elevator, probably trying to decide if his ears were playing tricks on him, or if Nick had said it. Before the guy could turn around, the elevator doors closed very quickly.

Chapter 2

Nick nodded to the doorman as he stepped onto the sidewalk and drew in a deep breath of stale morning air. The sound of a couple of distant sirens rose and fell almost in unison. Nick glanced around at the rows of parked cars along the sides of the dirty street, feeling sad that he hadn't been somehow magically transported to a

South Sea island while he slept.

Parked so closely to the car in front of it that there was no space to squeeze through, sat a pickup truck with a gun rack containing an AK-47 assault rifle and a bazooka. The car next to it was a bubbled three-wheeler with its front tire flat. Nick patted his pocket to make sure he still had his key, then walked past two more cars and started across the street. He saw only one slow-moving car nearby, and he returned his attention to looking at his own car as he approached it, wanting to make sure nothing had happened to it overnight.

That one slow-moving car, a fairly new Subarota Minx, held one passenger, an old lady wearing a beige hat.

The car was halfway down the block, cruising smoothly on autopilot as the driver knitted. Without warning, the car abruptly lurched forward, accelerating fast. The old woman missed a stitch.

The woman looked up in horror. She started to bang on the dash. "Oh no! Stop that! Stop it!"

The car barreled toward Nick, who walked in complete oblivion, wondering if that scratch near his front fender was new. Finally, with less than two car lengths left to go, Nick glanced toward the oncoming car, seeing its headlights flicker on and off as the car hit bumps in the road. He scrambled madly out of the way, barely managing to throw himself between two parked cars as the Subarota flashed past. An instant later, the car plowed into the string of parked cars. Sound died, leaving only the ticking of contracting metal and the dripping of fluid.

Nick got to his feet and dusted himself off. He trudged toward the wreck and muttered under his breath, "Man, I hate it when this happens."

He reached the wreck and pulled open the passenger door.

The old woman sagged forward, constrained by her seat belt. She seemed dazed, but fortunately the knitting needles had done no damage. Her eyes opened wider and she surveyed the view ahead, then looked up at Nick. "Oh no. My brand new car. It just – took off. I don't know what happened. I'm terribly sorry. It was an accident."

Nick glanced at the damaged cars. "No harm done." He turned to the doorman and yelled, "Call the cops, will you? We've got another runaway."

The doorman called back. "I just did. They're still on delayed reporting."

Nick nodded his understanding. Just as he turned back to the woman, the air bag controller belatedly activated, and the bag blew up in the woman's face, hammering her body backward into the seat. The air bag reached a knitting needle, and suddenly the bag exploded like an enormous balloon.

Nick hadn't heard anything that loud since he'd forgotten his earmuffs at the target practice range. The woman looked like she'd *never* heard anything that loud.

★   ★   ★

Several miles away, a midnight-blue van pulled out of an alley garage, which bore a sign saying, "Major Opportunity Business." The unmarked van knocked an old man and his shopping cart out of the way as it pulled onto the street.

★   ★   ★

Across town, a switch activated, and the automatic garage door on an expensive house rolled slowly upward. Ed Taylor walked forward, preoccupied, as the door rose. He avoided the bike lying in his path as he straightened his tie. Ed was a big man, with broad shoulders, a potbelly, and thinning hair.

If the garage door had worked properly, his head would have passed just under the bottom of the door. Instead, the door suddenly reversed just as Ed reached it, and his forehead smacked soundly against the descending edge.

"Damn it!" he said.

Ed struggled, pushing up on the door to get it to quit closing. Finally the door responded and started up again, resuming its interrupted path. Ed muttered and rubbed his forehead as he walked toward the rolled up newspaper lying near the front hedge. Behind him, the garage door continued rising without stopping, until finally the wood began to splinter and break under the constant pressure. A window popped loose from its surroundings and fell to the concrete, smashing thoroughly as it hit.

Oblivious, Ed stooped to grab his morning paper. Just as his fingers almost touched it, the paper jerked out of his reach. For the first time, Ed noticed that tied to the paper was a string leading into the hedge.

"Damn it, you kids. That's not funny!"

Watching from the window, Ed's son Alex grinned.

Ed took another step and reached for the paper again. It jerked away again. This time Ed moved faster, trying to reach it before the string yanked it away again. By now he was right next to the hedge.

Ed didn't get another chance to grab the paper. Suddenly a thick arm reached through the hedge and grabbed him, pulling him off-balance into the hedge.

On the other side of the hedge, Ed found no neighborhood children. Instead, two large, strong men met him. One of them, who sported large tattoos up and down both arms, had a small aerosol can stuck in one pocket. The other man had flaming red hair cut tent style. Ed's unsuccessful struggle lasted only seconds before they had him pinned to the ground. A second later a sweet-smelling spray in the face rendered him unconscious.

The two men manhandled him to a waiting midnight-blue van and dumped him inside. The tattooed man started the engine and made a U-turn.

The van's tires screeched as it lurched forward and sped away, narrowly missing a kid on a bike, and forcing the kid into a fence.

The red-haired man took a time card from a slot over the sun visor and looked at his digital watch before he filled in the next entry.

★   ★   ★

Nick Naught pulled onto the street. As he passed the next intersection, he saw down the side street a scene much like the one he had been in earlier. A runaway car crashed into a parked car as pedestrians scattered. Several nearby witnesses started to help, so Nick continued on his way.

Nick put his little finger in the ear that had been closest to the air bag explosion, and he wiggled the finger. He pulled the finger out, listened for a moment, and repeated the process.

A police car flashed past, siren on, lights flashing.

Nick turned his attention to the road ahead. "Radio on."

"Whatever you say," the car voice replied. The voice was feminine and sexy, with just a trace of huskiness.

The radio started playing some classical selection Nick didn't recognize. He banged his fist on the dash and the station switched to rock.

★   ★   ★

At a modest house in a different section of the city, Annette Taylor came out her front door. She was dressed for work, looking trim, and moving confidently. Today was going to be a good day. She had an appointment with her boss at the agency about the possibility of taking on a large, valued client.

In the front yard stood a very large tree. On Annette's side of the tree was a rolled up morning newspaper. On the other side of the tree were the two musclemen and the end of a string tied to the newspaper.

Annette spotted the paper. "Go get it, boy!" she called, and her collie raced out the front door and grabbed the newspaper. The string drew tight. The dog growled through clenched teeth. It knew *this* game. The dog shook its head from side to side and lowered its hindquarters, pedaling backward. The tug of war lasted only seconds before the string broke, and the dog rushed triumphantly inside with the paper, happy about the battle it had won, and not too curious about who had been defeated. Annette closed the door and started for her car.

One of the men pointed to the van. "Quick!"

The men raced to the van. The tattooed man started it up as Annette was starting her car. They pulled the van forward quickly, blocking the driveway, and the engine died.

In her rear-view mirror, Annette saw the two large men getting out of the midnight-blue van, guns in their hands. Without taking time to figure out why this was happening, and what they were after, she knew this wasn't a typical Monday. She twisted the wheel and goosed the engine. She almost mowed down the red-headed man as she raced around the van, knocking trash cans into the street.

The two men hopped into the van as Annette's car sped away. The driver flooded the engine as he tried to start it. The engine just spun slower and slower as the smell of gasoline filtered into the van and the squealing of Annette's car tires faded into the background.

★　　★　　★

Nick pushed through the revolving door into his office building lobby.

"Wanna buy a paper?" asked the newspaper vending machine. The machine's tone of voice gave the impression of hawking some illicit thrill.

"Sure," Nick said.

"That'll be six bucks."

Nick ran his credit card through the slot on top of the box. The machine's face opened, and, with a practiced motion, Nick snatched a paper just in time, as the lid snapped down *very* fast, like a bear trap.

"Have a nice day," said the vending machine.

As Nick waited for the elevator, a teenage boy in a striped shirt approached the coffee vending machine.

"I wouldn't bother, if I were you," Nick said.

The teenager ignored him and said to the machine, "Coffee, black."

Nick shrugged. As the elevator doors opened, the vending machine squirted coffee all over the kid's shirt and pants.

★   ★   ★

In Nick's unoccupied office, the phone began to ring. The phone answerer clicked on, and Nick's voice said, "Nick Naught private investigations. Leave a message. Unless you're with a collection agency." *Beep.*

"This is the Internal Revenue Service, Mr. Naught. Yesterday you missed your third audit appointment. Be in our office at two today, or a warrant will be issued for your arrest."

The phone answerer clicked off only seconds before Nick entered the office. He put the paper down on the desk and looked wistfully at the large South Seas island poster on his office wall. Finally he pressed a button on the phone answerer.

"Sorry," the answerer said. "No messages."

Nick sat down at his desk. The desk clock read 2:30 AM. He shook his head and pushed the clock slowly over the edge, where it landed with a *clunk* in his wastebasket.

★   ★   ★

Annette watched the elevator floor indicator stop. She leaned forward, anticipating the opening of the doors, but they stayed shut. She looked around to see if the elevator had an emergency bell switch.

Suddenly, in a voice mimicking the voice of a short, web-footed cartoon character almost always seen in a sailor suit with large buttons, the elevator hummed. It played the theme from "Twilight Zone." "Do do DO do. Do do DO do."

Annette banged on the control panel.

Finally, as the doors opened, the elevator voice laughed. "Wahhh. He he he he."

★ ★ ★

Annette knocked on the door saying "Nick Naught Private Investigations," then, without waiting for an answer, entered the office. She patted her hair into place, and glanced over her shoulder toward the elevator door in the hallway.

"Hello, Nick," she said.

Nick thought she looked sad, but she also looked determined, businesslike. Her hair was longer than he had seen it last, and the change looked good on her.

Nick got to his feet slowly, confused about why she would be here after all that had gone on between them. "Hello, Annette. I have to say I never really expected to see you here." Nick felt his insides start to churn, and he suddenly felt as forlorn as he had four years ago.

"I need your help," she said simply.

"After four years?"

Annette shook her head. "Let's not start in on it, all right? What's done is done. I wouldn't be here if I didn't figure I needed someone like you."

Nick was silent for a moment, considering. Finally he gestured at a chair. They both sat. "Okay. Today's business. Let's hear it."

Annette's calm facade crumbled a little, and she fidgeted. "Ed's been kidnapped. And someone tried to get me, too."

Nick leaned forward, concerned. "Why?"

"That's the worst part of all. I have absolutely no idea."

Nick caught his thoughts moving to the past, and he forced himself to think about the present. "I don't watch much television. Your brother's still a reporter for K-S-M-Y?"

Annette looked at him directly. Her eyes had a pained look Nick had seen before. "Yes. I already told them about it. Two big guys grabbed him this morning. One of the neighbors saw part of it out his window. They were probably the same two guys that were after me. Muscle guys I'd never seen before, one of them with lots of tattoos."

"I suppose you already called the police?"

"Sure. But they don't have time to do anything this month. They're too busy already."

Nick nodded and went through a mental checklist. "Did anything unusual happen recently? Did Ed meet a new woman, take out a big loan, buy a gun, take out insurance? Anything at all out of the ordinary that you know about?"

"Nothing. It's just been business as usual." She hesitated. "His wife is in the hospital, but I really don't see how that would relate to Ed being kidnapped — or to anyone coming after me."

"Anything else you can think of?"

"No, nothing. I put some of the things you might need in this envelope. His home address, things like that. And I wrote down descriptions of the two guys. Will you help?"

Nick sighed softly, not asking any of the questions he most wanted to ask. "Yeah. I've got a friend down at K-S-M-Y. Maybe he knows something that can get me started. I'll call him as soon as we're done talking."

Annette nodded. She seemed to have a hard time meeting Nick's gaze now. She glanced at the wall poster. "It looks so peaceful."

"Yes, it does. Which reminds me. My fee is a thousand a day, plus expenses. How about if you give me a retainer for a couple of days?"

Annette nodded again. She pulled out a credit card.

Nick took a charge card setup from a desk drawer. As he ran his company card and her card through, the machine spit his card across the room, where it landed in an in-box placed there to catch it. Nick walked over and retrieved the card. He handed her a receipt. "You still save your carbons?"

"Yes, please."

Nick started tearing out the little sheets of carbon paper. There must have been nearly twenty of them in the stack. Annette put them in a small card file she kept in her purse.

She managed to give him a level gaze. "Thanks, Nick."

"Where can I reach you?"

"You can't. I'm not about to go home now. I'll find a hotel and call you later."

Nick nodded. Annette rose and walked to the door. As she closed the door behind her, Nick looked up and sighed.

He shook his head, as if doing that would clear away the old thoughts, then picked up the phone. He dialed a *long* number.

"Thank you for using AT&T," said a voice on the line.

Then, "Thank you for using Sprint."

"Thank you for using MCI."

"Thank you for using U.S. West."

"I'm sorry. Your call cannot be completed. Please check the number and dial again."

"It must be some problem with AT&T."

"*Correction*. It must be some problem with *Sprint*."

Nick slapped his forehead. He felt tired. He put the receiver down, and tried again.

"Thank you for using AT&T."

"Thank you for using Sprint."

"Thank you for using MCI."

"Thank you for using U.S. West."

"Thank you for using Lucy's Phone Network."

"Hello. This is the President speaking."

Nick's head jerked up. "President of what?"

"Of the United States. Who is this?"

"Ah, sorry, sir. Wrong number."

Nick hung up. He rose and started for the door.

Chapter 3

In another part of the city sat a large office complex with a sign out front sporting block letters that said "Major Opportunity Business." Inside, two executives sat at a conference room table.

Mike McCormick, the company president, listened to the end of the briefing. He was a prematurely graying man with small gold earrings. The briefer was a senior company officer, Paula Rosenberg. She was about ten years his junior, and wore neither makeup nor earrings.

"That's fine," McCormick said when Rosenberg finished her old-business briefing. "Do it. Any new business?"

Rosenberg ran a finger down her list of notes. "Only one thing today. You remember David Turvey, the accountant who testified at the Williams trial?" As she spoke, she opened a notebook, extracted a photo, and slid it to McCormick. The photo was of a man in his sixties. Underneath the picture, large letters said, "David Turvey."

Rosenberg went on without waiting for an answer. "The Philadel-phia branch has verified that Turvey has definitely accepted a new identity and a disguise from the witness protection program. He's now here in town, using the name Nick Knott."

Rosenberg slid another photo to McCormick. The second photo was of the same man, but it showed an idiot mustache that looked like it had been just scribbled onto the photo with a large black marker. Underneath in large letters was, "Nick Knott."

"Your recommendation?" McCormick said. He looked at his watch.

"Send out a dispatch team. Have them do an analysis and com-plete the task. It should look like an accident."

"Fine. Is that it? I need to get to that charity luncheon."

★   ★   ★

Rosenberg leaned into Cynthia Willis's office door. "Willis, I need you to run a dispatch on a Nick Knott. An 'accidental.'"

"Can it wait 'til after break?" Willis asked. She had been just about to get up when Rosenberg arrived.

"Do it now, will you? It's for McCormick." Rosenberg started to leave.

"Gotcha. Is there a special charge number or just overhead?"

Too late. Rosenberg was already gone. Willis looked at her clock, which read "09:55" then quickly turned to her computer terminal. She grabbed a form and filled in a couple of blanks as she spoke to the terminal. "Give me a file on Nick Knott."

She rose impatiently, waiting on the machine. A moment later it spit a photograph out a slot in the side of the machine. The photo wasn't exactly like the one Rosenberg had had. The image was dif-ferent, and below the photo were several lines of small text headed in large letters with, "Nick Naught."

Willis grabbed the photo before it could fall into the wastebasket below the slot. She stapled the form to the photo and rushed out.

Only a moment after she had left, the computer spit out a different photo, the one for Nick Knott. The photo fell into the wastebasket.

★   ★   ★

Willis ran down the hall. She passed sections labeled "Accounts Terminating," "Numbers," "Security," "Laundry," and "Protection."

Don Lyeth was sitting at his desk when Willis rushed in and dumped the paperwork in his in-basket. Lyeth wore a bow-tie and had his shirtsleeves rolled up. His desk was perfectly neat, and even the two pieces of paper on top were lined up precisely parallel to the edge of the desk.

Willis started to leave. "Gotta run," she said.

"Hey, hey, hey. Not so fast," Lyeth said. He examined the form, then frowned like an auto mechanic with bad news.

"What's the problem?"

"What's this?" Lyeth asked. He shook the paper in the air. "We haven't used a form fifty-six for months."

"It's a dispatch. That's what I've always used."

"Not anymore. Form two-twelve." Lyeth slid a new form to her.

Willis scanned the paper and filled in a few of the blanks. "Okay. Look, I really gotta run."

"Not yet."

"What now?"

"You left the suspense date blank. And you didn't check 'accidental' or 'doesn't matter.'"

Willis filled in a date a week in the future and checked "accidental," then handed the form back. Lyeth examined the form for a full twenty seconds before he dropped it into another basket. "Okay then."

Chapter 4

NICK waited impatiently in the KSMY lobby. A receptionist with a cubed hairdo sat behind a desk and chewed gum. Next to the desk, a TV monitor showed the current live feed from the station, with news personalities Howard Darling and Connie Costanza. Through an adjacent glass wall, Nick could see the studio with Howard and Connie on the air. The red light on one of the cameras went on.

Howard started on cue. "And now, the kiss-my twelve o'clock news with Howard Darling and Connie Costanza." Howard was slightly pudgy, and his hair stuck out over his ears.

Connie took over. She was immaculately dressed and could have passed for a glamorous vid star, her straight black hair sparkling clean. "In the news today, three more air crashes in the United States and two abroad. A train derailed in New Jersey. Here at home there were almost fifty car accidents since this time yesterday. And today makes the 500th straight day of delayed accident reporting, nearing the record previously set about three years ago."

While Connie was talking, Howard was handed a note. He read it and was about to ask a question of someone off screen when he saw the camera was back on him and Connie had finished.

Howard stumbled. "Er — I've just been handed a special bulletin. Please stand by." Howard put on a nonchalant air and showed the note to Connie as he pointed to a word.

"Subpoena," Connie whispered.

Howard brightened. He took the note back and began to read. "In an unprecedented act, the Justice Department today issued over twenty su*bp*oenas to descendants of the group of decision-makers originally responsible for the breakup of the telephone company."

During Howard's story, Connie seemed to have a sudden urge

to scratch her nose. Nick was positive she was trying to suppress a grin at Howard's mispronunciation. Howard's gaze flicked toward her, and a frown crinkled his forehead. He resumed the story and was almost finished when his watch alarm sounded. He tried to unobtrusively turn it off, but in the process he knocked over his glass of water. Instantly, like a cat caught making an error, he assumed a blank expression that said, "What's the problem? I didn't do anything."

Connie shook her head sadly. Howard caught sight of the motion from the corner of his eye. He glanced at her, and she abruptly stopped and smiled innocently.

As Howard resumed, his wristwatch started to give off smoke, but he didn't notice it. "Also in the news today, researchers at UCLA have been tracking the spread of a new AIDS-like virus within the animal community. So far, the deadly virus has showed up only in cows, lambs, and sheep, but today it was announced that the scientists have discovered the virus in alligators." Howard hesitated before he capped the story with his pronouncement. "GatorAIDS."

The news director looked incredulously at Howard, and he smacked his palm against his forehead.

Howard suddenly realized his watch was smoking. He panicked. In the process of trying to get it off his wrist, he fell over backward.

As the station went promptly to a rat chow commercial, a door opened, and Earle Thompson came in and greeted Nick. "Sorry to keep you waiting. Come on in." Earle's nose was large enough, and his glasses rims dark enough, and his mustache black enough, that from a distance he seemed to be wearing a Groucho Marx disguise.

Nick followed Earle past several news people at their desks busily keying in stories. From the computer terminals came various video game noises.

Past the bullpen, a corridor led into a walled area with private offices. From the room ahead, came a short, loud buzz.

Nick glanced in as they passed the office. Next to the door was a name tag saying, "Jim Curtis." Curtis looked like a fairly normal guy in his thirties, but he was adjusting a collar with a little black box stuck on it. As they passed, Curtis shut his office door.

Nick and Earle took seats in the next office, which was Earle's. Earle was a real sportsman. Hanging on his wall were mementos: a tennis racquet with a broken head and a golf club with a bent shaft.

Nick tilted his head toward the Curtis's office. "I feel kinda wasted as a private eye. I didn't know you vid guys got to wear dog collars."

"Cute. But it's not a dog collar. You ever drive a long way on manual? Get a little drowsy? Your head tilts too far forward, like you're going to sleep? That's when those things buzz real loud and wake you up."

Nick shook his head. "Boy, I could have used one of those in school. Listen, I won't take up much of your time. I'm trying to get a lead on who might have grabbed Ed Taylor, or why."

"A friend must have hired you. I can't imagine the police are getting too excited, or them finding the budget to hire independents."

"What can you tell me?"

From the next room came the brief sound of a buzzer. Earle ignored it. "I don't know. Ed lived for work. The little time he did have free, he spent with his kid, Alex, or using his computer. I think he fancies himself a hacker."

"What's he been working on lately? Anything that could account for someone grabbing him?"

"I really doubt it. He's been doing some routine funding profiles. Nothing special."

From the office next door came another burst of the buzzer.

Nick looked at his watch. "Can I take a look at Ed's office?"

"Sure thing. It's right down this way."

As they left Earle's office, the buzzer next door started again. This time it just kept on going and going forever.

Down the hall four doors, Earle said, "Here it is. I'll leave you to it. Good luck."

"Thanks. I may need it."

"You know, Nick, I hope you don't mind me saying this, but you don't look too happy. Is Ed a real good friend?"

Nick hesitated. "It's not that. It's his sister, Annette. She hired me. I hadn't seen her for about four years." Nick looked away. "Since she walked out on me."

Earle nodded. "Well, best of luck on both counts." He left Nick in the office and closed the door behind him.

Nick sat down at Ed's desk and opened the front drawer. He pulled out a sandwich that looked like it had been left there when the building was built. He dropped the sandwich into the trash can. He looked farther into the drawer, using a ruler to move stuff aside.

He flipped through a stack of paper on top of the desk and found nothing obvious.

Empty handed, Nick walked back toward the entrance. As he passed Jim Curtis's office, with its door closed, the buzzer was still going. Nick glanced around to see if anyone was looking. He rapped the door once with the tip of his shoe, hard. The buzzer stopped for a moment, then resumed.

Chapter 5

THE air was muggy as Nick walked out of KSMY. Just down the street, a man parked in a luxury car with power seats was slowly being crushed into the ceiling by the rising seat. Nick moved to help, but at the last minute, the man managed to get the seat to stop rising, and he proceeded to crawl out the window.

Nick started across the street, wondering which universal law covered always having to park on the other side of the street from where he was going, and wondering how all the people on *this* side had somehow received exemptions. He had just emerged between two parked cars, when a sludge-brown Dodge truck with yellow smog-lights just down the street suddenly began to accelerate fast. By this time of day, Nick was wide awake, and he noticed the car while it was still several car lengths away. He scrambled. He dived between two parked cars just before the Dodge plowed into one of them.

Nick picked himself off the ground and walked toward the damaged car, thinking that maybe most cars should be named "Dodge."

Behind the wheel was a guy who needed a shave and possessed a nose that looked red from too much alcohol or sunburn. Before Nick arrived, the man quickly switched a control on the dash, and a dash sign changed from *manual* to *autopilot engaged*.

Nick pulled open the driver-side door.

The driver looked up at Nick. "Man, are you okay? I'm sorry. This thing just went out of control. What a mess."

Nick looked down at his dusty pants. "I'm fine. This keeps me in shape, and it's not nearly as annoying as jogging. How about you?"

The driver looked at his face in the rear-view mirror and touched his nose. "I'll be okay. I'm just a little dazed."

"Aren't we all?" Nick muttered. "Say, you'd probably better get out of there pretty fast."

"Why, what's the —"

The man's words were cut off as the Dodge's air bag finally blew up in his face. This bag must have had the large, economy-size gas canister, because it blew up so far that it knocked Nick backward before it exploded.

★   ★   ★

Nick drove along a business street. A bump in the road switched the radio to classical. Nick banged on the dash, and the station switched back to rock. He wiggled his finger inside one ear, then hit the heel of his hand against the side of his head.

An ambulance flashed past, siren on, lights flashing.

As Nick drove by an apartment building, a man on the sidewalk in a powered wheelchair was suddenly accelerated to warp speed and rammed into a collection of trashcans.

He knew he was getting close to the school, because he passed "Guns 'R' Us." On the right, was a building with the sign, "Hackers' Savings and Loan."

A few blocks later, Nick pulled up in front of Burbank High School.

Nick's footsteps echoed as he walked down the hall and passed by a silent large box with lights, a lens, and a speaker grill on the front. The box bore the legend, "Hall Monitor." The speaker grill suddenly came alive. "May I see your hall pass, please?"

Nick stopped and patted his pockets. "Sorry, I must have left it in my other pants." He started walking again.

"No, no, no! No one without a hall pass is allowed beyond this checkpoint."

"Sorry. I'm in a hurry. I'm not even a student."

Suddenly the hallway was filled with the sound of a machine gun spraying bullets everywhere, mixed with the sound of heavy artillery. Nick pulled his gun and crouched. Only an instant later, he realized the sounds came from the hall monitor, and he'd been had.

"Just kidding," said the hall monitor as Nick moved closer, his gun still in his hand.

"Boy, you sure got me on that one. What a riot. Ha ha ha."

Nick started to walk away again, and, as he left, he kicked the hall monitor wall-plug loose from the wall-socket. The machine gun noises started up again, but quickly dropped in pitch and volume until the hall monitor was quiet.

"Just kidding," Nick said, and he smiled. That was probably the best time he'd ever had in a school.

Two corridors away, Nick stopped at a room bearing the sign, "Room 156, Science." He peeked around the corner into the room. A bunch of bored high-schoolers sat in desks, listening inattentively to the science teacher, an old lady who could have been teaching when Nixon was in school. She wore black shoes with large, raised heels.

"All right," the science teacher said. "Who can tell me why mountain ranges exist? Anyone."

Several students scrutinized their desktops. A pimply over-achiever raised his hand.

"Yes, Danny?"

"The — ah — mountain ranges were formed by the great flood. Noah's flood."

A couple of the students looked vaguely skeptical. Several of the others looked comatose. Nick cringed.

"Danny, that's exactly right. Now what else is the Genesis flood responsible for?" Before anyone could raise a hand, the science teacher noticed Nick. "Yes, may I help you?"

"I hope so. I need to talk to Alex Taylor."

The science teacher hesitated. "Are you a drug dealer?"

Nick looked over his shoulder to see if anyone was behind him. He shook his head and held up one hand in a Boy Scout salute.

"All right, Alex. But no more than five minutes."

Alex Taylor rose and came out to the hall. He was a gangly kid, chewing gum. His brown hair stuck straight out from his skull at every point, as though his head contained a large static generator instead of a brain nearly the size of a hamster's.

Nick said, "I'm trying to find out where your father might be, Alex."

"Why, what's he done?"

Nick frowned. "He was kidnapped. Didn't anyone tell you?"

"Oh, yeah. Right." Alex looked around. "Well, he ain't here." He jammed his hands into his pockets.

"Uh — yeah. Total agreement. You got any idea at all where he might be?"

"Have you looked at kiss-my? He works there. Maybe they took him there."

"I've been there."

"You know, you could just turn on the TV. He's there a lot, and you just might see him."

Nick sighed. "Yeah, well, Alex, you've been a very big help. Really. Thanks very much." He started to walk away, but Alex called after him.

"Hey, I got three more minutes."

"That's great. Probably you should lie down for a minute. I can imagine this has probably been a pretty grueling experience for you."

Nick left Alex behind and continued down the hall. The next room was labeled "Algebra," and the teacher was talking solemnly to his class. "We are gathered here together to talk about a subject *He* would have wanted you all to learn well. Yes, I'm talking about *algebra*. Yea verily, I say unto you..."

Nick shook his head and kept on walking. The next room, labeled "Physics," was noisy even before he reached it. Instead of having desks, the students sat in pews. The teacher was shouting in a rich, pulpit voice. "E equals M C squared! Do you believe?"

The class shouted in unison, "We believe!"

Nick wiggled a finger in one ear and tapped on the side of his head. If there was anything he believed in, it was garbage-in, garbage-out. He took the turn into the lobby. There a glass case held a picture of the school mascot, a penguin. Next to it sat a confessional booth.

Through the glass walls to the principal's office, Nick saw the principal pacing in a circle. The rosy-cheeked man wore a bishop's hat and a red robe, and held a scepter.

Outside, the air felt clammy. Nick walked down the sidewalk, trying to decide what to do next. He was almost to his car when, down the street, a car exploded, and nearby people started toward it. Nick shook his head and got into his car. He sat there a minute before he finally put the key in the ignition.

"Your seat belt is unfastened," the car said. Its tone seemed possessive and protective.

Nick fastened his seat belt.

"Your door isn't latched."

Nick opened the door and slammed it shut.

"Your fly is open."

Nick looked down.

"Made you look."

★   ★   ★

As Nick drove, a fire truck flashed passed him, siren on.

Minutes later, as he sat stopped at a school crossing, another runaway car, this one speeding straight through the crossing, sent children running for safety in all directions. A youthful crossing guard gave the runaway car a rude gesture.

A school bus parked on the street had its doors clamped tight on a squirming school kid. The kid frantically kicked his legs, which dangled out the door.

Chapter 6

NICK pulled into a parking space in front of the hospital across the street. The parking meter read, "Violation" until Nick banged the meter sideways with his fist. The violation flag went down, setting the meter to, "One Hour."

Nick winced as a teenage girl with an incredibly loud boom box passed the nearby "Quiet Zone" sign. She walked by three cars in a row, and the windows in each car shattered at the sound.

On the sidewalk sat a vending machine bearing the label, "Malpractice Insurance."

"Hey, buddy," said the machine. "You got the right time?"

"Yeah. It's about one."

"Thanks. You going in for an operation?"

"Nope."

"Never mind."

Inside, Nick was walking past the emergency desk when a paramedic rolled in an injured woman.

"I'm afraid this one's a croaker," the paramedic said to the nurse. He glanced around the room as though he had other things on his mind.

The nurse stood up fast and put her hands on her hips. "Who do you think you are? God? It's not for you to casually decide if that patient lives or dies. That's what doctors are for."

As the paramedic wheeled the patient away, the patient lifted her head up weakly and gave the paramedic an obscene gesture.

Nick approached the nurse. "I'm looking for Carla Taylor."

"Why? What's she done?" The nurse looked suspicious.

"Nothing that I know of. I'm just here to visit her."

"Up the stairs around the corner that way. Room 350."

Nick started for the stairs. All the way to the corner, he could feel the nurse's stare in the middle of his back. Feeling more comfortable after he had left her sight, he peered into an operating room. A team of gowned people stood around the operating table, watching the doctor as she held a scalpel and she carefully cut into the patient. The doctor's digital wrist watch alarm went off, and she instinctively moved her hands to turn it off.

Blood spurted an amazing distance out of the patient's body, and everyone got really busy, especially the guy who got squirted in the face.

Carla Taylor's room was a double. According to the note outside the door, she occupied the bed nearest the door. Another patient was apparently asleep in the other bed despite the television being on. Next to the far bed stood a man trying to open a bottle of pills.

On the television was a newsbreak with Howard and Connie.

Howard said, "Another offshore oil rig leak has been detected at a Mogo platform in the Pacific. It went unnoticed for almost two weeks due to the already high levels of oil in that region." He was no longer wearing his digital watch.

Connie continued, "OPEC, the Oil Producing and Extorting Countries, issued a statement condemning the pollution. Our roving reporter, Melanie Wortham, is on the scene of the latest spill."

The view switched to Melanie. She stood on a dark substance. "Mogo issued a public apology today, and have stated that cleanup crews will be reaching the area you can see here as soon as they finish the cleanup operations in the Potomac. Like, this is Melanie Wortham, speaking to you from four miles off the coast of California. Really."

Melanie walked toward the camera. Her smile tightened as her feet came loose from the dark substance with a soft sucking sound only after much resistance, and it became obvious that she was standing on solidified oil sludge. A small dirty child was building a castle in the sludge. Near the child, two sun-bathers lay on towels that showed the oil seeping through. Beyond them, a sign said, "Keep off the water."

Carla Taylor switched the television off with the remote control. The TV turned itself on again, so Carla had to turn it off a second time. She watched the set intently for a moment before looking up. She was a redhead, her hair done in the spiky curls that was more fashionable among teenagers. She looked sleepy.

"Carla Taylor?" Nick said.

"Yes."

"I'm Nick Naught. Your husband's sister hired me to try to find him since the police are so busy. I thought perhaps you could help me."

Carla's attention was suddenly caught by the man standing next to her roommate's bed. He was still trying unsuccessfully to open a prescription bottle, and the child-proof cap was really getting to him. He began to get really energetic, and finally he shouted, "Damn it all!"

As his face turned red, the man gave it one more tremendous effort. The cap suddenly came off the bottle, and pills went flying. In an effort to save a few of the pills, he lunged and accidentally rammed the over-the-bed tray against the bed, where, despite his efforts to save it, a pitcher of water flooded onto the patient. The patient, a young girl, sat up suddenly and was caught in the forehead by the man's elbow as he swiveled. The girl was knocked out cold.

"Who's that?" Nick asked.

"That's Dr. Kennedy. My surgeon."

Nick took a deep breath, wishing he had read the fine print on his health maintenance plan and wishing he knew where he would be admitted if the occasion arose. He asked, "What are you in for?"

"Well, at first I just wanted to have a wart removed. But we got to talking, and I signed up for this new procedure to improve my memory. It was just a twenty-minute operation, and I'm almost fully recovered already. It's supposed to improve my short-term memory, my long-term memory, my learning rate, and — did I mention short-term memory?"

"Yes. You did."

"And did I mention short-term memory?"

"Mrs. Taylor, I need to ask you —"

"Why did you call me Mrs.?"

Nick felt sick. "This isn't going to work, is it?"

"I don't think so. Er — what isn't going to work?"

"Just lie quietly. I hope I didn't upset you." Nick started to leave.

"Yes, I'm fine," Carla said.

Dr. Kennedy, still cleaning up, dropped the pitcher on his toe. He used some words Nick had never heard before, and Nick wondered if they were medical jargon.

Nick retraced his path, feeling unproductive. In another operating room he passed, a medical team surrounded a patient on the operating table. The heart monitor was *beeping* at the right interval, but suddenly it stopped. The medical team began to pack it in.

The patient's head rose. He looked panicked at seeing everyone leaving. He looked over at the heart monitor that said he was dead. His mouth worked soundlessly. He clutched his chest and fell back to the table, apparently dead. The heart monitor started *beeping* again.

As Nick exited the hospital, a meter-person had just reached his car. The meter still said "One hour." The meter-person pulled out a small rubber mallet and whacked the meter lightly. The "Violation" flag came back up, and the meter-person proceeded to write a ticket.

As Nick took the ticket and got into his car, the meter-person grinned and made one hand into a gun, as though to say gotcha.

Chapter 7

NICK kept a frequent watch on the rear-view mirror as he drove, not wanting to be rear-ended by an emergency vehicle. He passed First Chapel of Elvis. For a weekday, it looked fairly busy. A group of four people in white pants with sequins were just going inside.

Nick caught the flashing light in the rear-view mirror in time to pull to the right. A car flashed past, red lights spinning, its siren on. On the side of the car was a sign saying, "Pizza."

Nick gained on a tanker truck bearing a sign saying, "Caution, Nuclear Waste." From the back of the truck leaked a steady stream of brown fluid. Nick pulled out far enough to see the reflected view of the driver, who wore a gas mask and headphones. Nick slowed down to give the truck lots of space and tried to keep his wheels straddling the flow.

Minutes later, as he neared the office, he approached an intersection showing a green light.

Approaching the same intersection, from the cross street, was a large truck. The traffic light for the truck was green also. Nick's car grew closer and closer to the intersection, maintaining full speed. Finally it was obvious to the truck driver that Nick's car was not stopping for the light. The driver gave the horn a long blast.

At the sound of the horn, Nick took his eyes away from the rear-view mirror, and suddenly realized the truck was about to broadside him. He jammed on the brakes. His car skidded sideways, and the truck sped past, just missing Nick's bumper.

Nick yelled, "Idiot!" As he yelled, he heard the truck driver call him something even less flattering.

The car said, "Take it easy, big boy."

Nick pulled over to assess the damage. From where he parked, he could see the light from both directions. It was green in both. As he watched, one direction went instantly from green to red, and a pick-up truck had to slam on its brakes.

In a van parked in a near-by parking lot, Dennis Cotton, the red-nosed man who had almost hit Nick earlier in the day, watched as Nick got out of his car and walked around it. Dennis raised a car phone to his mouth. "Damn it! I thought we had him."

Dennis hung up, started the van engine, and headed toward the exit. On his way out of the parking lot, he saw a shiny car parked diagonally and taking up two parking spots. With only the barest hesitation, Dennis deliberately veered close and creased the car door with his bumper. Satisfied at having done *something* productive this time, he said, "I always wanted to do that."

★   ★   ★

On the way through his building lobby, Nick passed a man with his hand stuck in the newspaper vending machine. The guy tried unsuccessfully to get loose, as the doorman looked for the right tool to fix the problem. Nick waited for the elevator, the lobby too noisy for his taste because a customer was banging on the coffee machine.

★   ★   ★

In Nick's empty office, the phone rang, and the phone answerer clicked on. "Nick Naught private investigations. Mr. Naught is out of the office, making the world safe for capitalism and the IRS, so please leave a message." *Beep*.

"Nick Naught. Nick Naught, who's there? Sorry. I shouldn't do that. Mr. Naught, this is the lottery commission. Our records show you have a winning ticket. You need to produce it by five today to claim the five million dollars. Please call us."

Not five seconds after the phone answerer clicked off, Nick

entered the office. He pressed a button on the phone answerer, and the machine said, "Sorry. No messages."

Nick sat down at his desk. He picked the clock out of the wastebasket. It still read 2:30 AM. He dropped it back in.

The phone rang, and he picked it up. "Hello."

The phone answerer message started up again. "Nick Naught private —"

"I've *got* it," Nick said.

"Sorry. You don't have to yell."

Annette's voice came on the line. "I'm glad I caught you, Nick. I wondered if you'd found out anything yet."

Nick looked at his watch. "To tell you the truth, this case is going a little slower than normal. I've checked at the office and with his wife and son. They both must have had a few knots in the old umbilical cord."

"Maybe there's something at the house that would help. I could meet you there."

"All right. But I'm starved, so I'm going to swing by Big Burger. Meet you at the house in an hour and a half?"

"Right."

A moment after Nick hung up, the phone rang again. Nick picked it up. "Hello."

The phone answerer message started up again. "Nick Naught private —"

"I've *got* it."

The answerer said, "I knew that."

"Mr. Naught, this is G. David Chamness. I've been trying to establish contact with you for days. We communicated last week regarding my client's impending suit identifying you as the defendant." In the lawyer's office, his desk stretched almost the full width of his office. Behind him was a wall-to-wall, floor-to-ceiling bookcase entirely filled with books with identical bindings.

"Hang on a minute, okay?" Nick opened a desk drawer and retrieved an auto translator with one knob and a screen on it. The screen currently said, "French." Nick set the device on top of the desk, attached a cord to the phone, and turned the knob. The screen changed rapidly to "German," then to "Doctor," "Politician," "Punk," and finally to "Lawyer."

Nick said, "Don't you think 'impending suit' is a little strong? 'Petty harassment' would be closer."

"I don't think you fully appreciate the enormous gravity of the circumstances in which you find yourself enveloped."

The auto-translator screen said, "I'm serious."

Nick leaned back. "Can you speak up? The connection is fading."

"My client proposes to prosecute to the maximum extent of the pertinent statutes."

The auto-translator screen said, "He wants everything he can get."

"I'm having trouble taking this whole thing seriously. I mean the guy was holding up a convenience store. He had a gun. The owner and a customer can back up my story. And can you speak louder? This connection is terrible."

The lawyer's raised his voice to nearly a shout. "In actual point of fact, the weapon in question was a facsimile, one fabricated from molded plastic and acquired at a K-Mart."

The auto-translator screen said, "The gun was fake."

"Sure. But how was I to know that? And can you speak louder?"

The lawyer was actually shouting by now. "That's precisely my contention. You were not apprised of the full extent of the situation. Yet you proceeded to wound the plaintiff with a projectile weapon."

The auto-translator screen said, "You shot him."

"What? Louder."

The lawyer sounded near apoplexy from shouting so loud. "You willfully caused my client substantial pain and suffering by your wanton disregard for his unalienable rights."

The auto-translator screen said, "He missed a hot date. His toe hurts. And he didn't get the money."

Nick was enjoying himself. He had the telephone receiver held at arm's length. He brought the mouthpiece closer and muffled his voice with his hand. "I'm having a devil of a time hearing you. Maybe you should call back on another line."

"All right. I will do just that."

Nick hung up the phone and walked out the door. Behind him the phone began to ring.

Chapter 8

THE sun had almost broken through the smog as Nick drove. A police car overtook him and flashed past with its siren on. Not five seconds later, another police car flashed past, siren on, going the *opposite* direction.

Nick drove through a neighborhood so poor that all the houses had satellite dishes in the *front* yards.

Nick was on schedule when he pulled into the restaurant parking. In a car next to the drive-in speaker, a customer screamed, "Burger and fries!"

From the speaker grill came a heavily garbled, "What?"

The customer burned rubber leaving the drive-in window.

Nick parked well away from the drive-in exit and went inside.

He was examining the menu on the table when a disturbing shadow fell over the tabletop. The shadow seemed to be a person with a gun in one hand. Nick flinched. He looked up and saw Annette with her handbag. The gun shadow had just been a trick of the light. Annette's gaze took in the shadow and Nick's reaction. She maneuvered her fingers and made a shadow of an AK-47 assault rifle.

Annette said, "I had to go this same way, so I thought I'd join you. Is that all right?"

"It's still a free country." Nick traced a line with one finger on the counter top. "And I suppose company wouldn't hurt. These fast food places always seem so sterile to me."

Behind Nick a waiter dropped a sandwich on the floor, picked it up, dusted it off, and continued nonchalantly on his way.

Annette looked at the menu. "I know what you mean. It's like you could eat off the floor."

"You know what you want?"

Annette looked at Nick just a little too long before she glanced back at the menu. "Sure. Do you?"

"Yeah." Nick pressed a button near the speaker grill. He wondered if Annette's hesitation might have meant she had some second thoughts about leaving him. They had argued more than he had liked, but when things were going smoothly he had felt more comfortable than he ever had, before or after. He said nothing, and tried to suppress the thoughts. Why torment himself? Probably she had just been deciding between the Golden Bun and the Biggie Burgie.

A moment later the order taker replied in a voice garbled almost beyond recognition. "Are you ready to order?"

"Yes. We'd like one —" he looked where Annette pointed on the menu "— number twelve and a coffee. And one number eight and a glass of water."

The order taker hesitated. "What?"

Nick faced the microphone and spoke slowly. "One number

twelve and a coffee. And one number eight and a glass of water."

"What?"

Nick sighed. "Never mind." To Annette he said, "I'll be back."

Nick rolled up his sleeves and rose. He walked back to the counter where sign said, "Manual Orders." There was a line.

A few minutes later, Nick carried a tray back to the table. As he passed a teenager at the serve-yourself drink refill station, the machine shot a couple of ice cubes in an arc. The teenager backed up, trying to catch them in the cup, and ran into a restaurant employee carrying a large stack of trays. The employee was knocked off balance. He staggered toward a nearby swinging door, struggling to keep the trays from falling. Just as everything appeared under control, another employee came through the swinging doors fast enough to knock the trays over. The trays fell and spread out over half the area of the floor.

A customer at an automatic coffee dispenser paid no attention to the clatter, but instead stared at the brown sludge oozing into his cup.

Nick reached the table and sat down. "All taken care of. This sure is a noisy place."

"A lot noisier than some South Seas island would be, huh?"

"Oh, the poster in my office?"

"Yes. I take it you'd rather be there?"

"What, rather be in my office?" Nick asked. "No, I know you mean on an island. There are times when the idea's really appealing. I've started to have this recurring dream about a sailboat in water so clean you can put your hand in it."

"That does sound nice." Annette inspected her meal. "Where did we go wrong, Nick?"

"I really wish I knew." He looked at her, but she wouldn't meet his gaze.

From a speaker at a nearby table the order taker's loud voice said, "What?" The person at that table got up and started toward the manual order counter.

*   *   *

Dusk was coming on as Nick and Annette exited the restaurant. The sun no longer had the energy to punch through the smog, but it made a brownish-yellow glow in the west.

"We could just take my car to your brother's house," Nick said.

"Sure."

Nick walked in silence, irritated at himself for letting his mind drift to the way things had been before she walked out.

Nick tried his key in the lock, but it didn't work. He frowned and looked up.

He had stopped at the wrong car. This one, although the identical model, belonged to someone else. His car was right next to it.

After opening the right door, Nick held it for Annette, then walked around to his side. The engine stared smoothly.

The breathy car voice said, "Your headlights are off."

Nick turned on the headlights.

"You're low on gas."

Nick tapped the digital gauge.

"So. Who's the bimbo?"

Annette gave Nick a slow, hard stare.

Moments after they had driven away, the owner of the car next to Nick's returned. He got in and turned his key in the ignition. The engine didn't start, but instead the car began to fill with blue slime. The man banged on the car door and windows, but he couldn't get out.

Chapter 9

NICK finished pumping gas, and pulled out the self-serve pump nozzle. The price per gallon on the pump read $7.50, and he had put over $200 into the car. As Nick hung up the nozzle, he thumped the gas pump dial, and it dropped to $150.

He put the gas cap back on as the car voice belched. "Excuse me."

Nick shook his head and fed his credit card into the machine next to the pump.

Two stations down from Nick, a young guy with a digital watch pumped gas into a General Nippon Tracer. His watch beeped, and he reflexively pulled his arm toward him, pumping gas all over himself in the process.

Nick got back in the car and drove off. Ten seconds later, a van pulled through in his wake. Driving the van was the tattooed strong guy who had been after Annette. As he began to accelerate after Nick, the driver flipped a lit cigarette out his window. From behind him came a *whoomp!* Dazzling light reflected off the shiny surfaces, and from somewhere in the brilliance came a startled *Yelp!*

★   ★   ★

Streetlights were lit as Nick and Annette traveled along a residential street. Darkness had brought little relief from the heat.

Annette took a deep breath. "What a beautiful night."

Down a side street, a car careened out of control.

The car said, "It's thirty-one degrees Celsius."

Nick looked over at Annette. "Yeah, it sure is."

"A light wind is out of the southwest," said the car.

Annette raised her eyebrows. "Am I imagining things, or does your car seem a little jealous?"

"An automobile? Don't be silly."

The car said, "That's telling her, Nick."

★　★　★

Nick and Annette pulled up near Ed Taylor's house. Nick couldn't park directly in front of the house because the automatic, over-watering-proof sprinkler system was busily spraying the street. Not a drop was going on the grass. Nick and Annette got out and started up the driveway.

Annette said, "I should be able to get us by the security system. I made arrangements for their son to stay with friends until Carla gets out of the hospital or we find Ed."

"Probably not in that order."

A lighted panel next to the front door held a keypad. Above it was a speaker grille for the voice-operated house-security system.

"Hello," said the gravel-voiced security system.

"Hello," said Annette. To Nick, she said, "First you have to key in the right sequence. Then it will ask for a password." She typed in a five-digit number.

The security system said, "Sorry. Try it again."

Annette looked puzzled. She tried the number again.

"No. Try it again." The security system sounded testy.

Annette tried the number again.

Irritated this time, the security system said, "Come on. Try it again."

Annette tried the number again.

"Give me a bugging break! It's five eight five one four."

Annette tried the new number.

"Very good! Now what's the blasted password?"

Annette whispered, "Film at eleven."

"What?"

Annette raised her voice slightly. "Film at eleven."

"What?'

Annette looked flustered at the idea of yelling the secret password into the quiet night air. She looked around.

Nick nudged her aside and hit his flattened palm hard against the speaker grill.

"Welcome!" said the security system. The door latch clicked and the door swung open.

Nick and Annette walked slowly into the dark foyer.

"I just had a thought," Nick said. "They don't have a dog, do they?"

"No. Just a cat."

Even while Annette spoke, the cat cried out as Nick stepped on its tail.

By the time Annette flicked on a light switch, the cat had already scampered to safety.

They walked cautiously into the tidy kitchen and flipped on the light switch. A sudden *whir* from a blender near the sink came on with the light.

Nick flipped the light off. The blender went off.

Nick flipped the light on. The blender *whir* started again.

Nick and Annette relaxed a little. Nick went over to the blender. He turned it off and simultaneously the toaster ejected two burned pieces of toast.

In the living room, Annette flipped on the light switch. At the phone answerer, Nick paused and pushed the button.

"Four messages," The answerer said.

Beep.

"Hey, Alex, this is Richard. I've got a problem with number eight on the geometry homework. When you worked it out, how many angels did you think could dance on the head of a pin?"

Beep.

"Mr. Taylor, this is Michelle Clark at the library. I've had to re-shelve the computer books you've been working with. If you need them again, just ask."

Beep.

"Alex, I just wanted to remind you to do your homework. I'll be home soon. Love, Mom."

Beep.

"Alex, I just wanted to remind you to do your homework. I'll be home soon. Love, Mom."

Nick shook his head.

Nick and Annette moved into another room and approached a table covered with computer equipment, including a modem and a telephone. The computer was off.

Nick said, "This looks like an expensive collection of equipment."

"He's serious about his hobby."

They searched the stacks of printouts on the table, finding nothing that looked like it could help.

As they continued the search in another room, Annette said, "I've heard Ed talk about a wall safe. I wonder where it might be."

"We could try there." Nick pointed at a wall adorned with several small paintings. All but one were reasonably positioned. The odd one was over-large. It hung right in the upper corner of the room and featured a picture of a wall safe.

They swung the picture aside and exposed a *wall-safe*!

"Well, well," Nick said. "What do we have here?"

"A wall safe," the safe said.

Nick turned to Annette. "Any idea of the combination?"

"Sorry," she said.

"What's your brother's birthday?"

"July 30, 1975."

Nick tried 7-30-75.

"Sorry," said the safe. "Try again."

Nick said, "What's Carla's birthday?"

"Uh, March 26, same year."

Nick tried the new combination.

"Missed it by *that* much," the safe said.

"Which number was wrong?"

"You don't think I'm so stupid that I'm going to tell you the combination is seventy-five, three, twenty-six do you?"

Nick and Annette grinned at each other. Nick tried the new combination and the safe opened.

Nick pulled out the contents. The safe contained nothing but issues of 1990's comic books. "Mom isn't going to throw these babies out, huh?"

In the kitchen on the way out, Annette said, "I can't believe it. We couldn't even find the cat. And we know *it's* here."

"Maybe we can learn something at the library. And forget the cat. I'm sure it's just fine.

They moved into the foyer and turned out the light. As they walked the two feet to the front door, something slid under Nick's foot, and the cat cried out again.

★   ★   ★

Nick and Annette pulled away from the Taylor house. The sprinkler was still watering the street. Little sensors stuck into the soil were undoubtedly sending the message that the lawn hadn't had enough water yet.

In the distance, an engine started up and headlights flicked on. The van from the gas station reversed direction and started to follow, but just as the van was going in the right direction, a dog walked into the street and sat down right in front of the van's headlights.

The van stopped suddenly, and the driver honked the horn. The dog stayed right where it was.

Chapter 10

NICK passed a parked police car.

Only seconds later, the police car came to life, lights on, motor racing, and it started to follow. Its siren came on.

Nick's car said, "Fuzz at six o'clock."

Nick looked in the rear-view mirror and saw the flashing lights. "What now?" He looked at Annette and pulled over.

The police car stopped three car lengths back.

The cop driving got out of his door, and crouched behind it, gun drawn.

The second cop looked over from the passenger seat. He finished munching a donut and threw the box in the back seat with the rest of the boxes. He looked over at his partner and said, "You know, he can still shoot your feet." He licked his fingers.

The first cop climbed back in the car and angled his gun out the window left-handedly. He pulled a bullhorn out and tried to use it at the same time, sticking his head out the window awkwardly. "This is the police. Get out of the car. Lean against it with your hands spread."

Nick and Annette opened their respective doors and got out. They leaned against Nick's car, hands spread obediently.

The cops cautiously approached, weapons drawn. One cop covered each of them.

"I need to see your driver's license, sir," the first cop said.

"It's in my wallet in my back pocket. What's this all about, officer?"

"Our database shows your car as a stolen vehicle. Suspects armed and dangerous. The database said to shoot on sight, so don't test your luck."

"There's got to be some mistake. Does she look dangerous to you?" Nick hesitated. "Okay, don't answer that."

The cop retrieved the wallet, and looked at the license. "Just a minute, please." He gestured for the other cop to cover them both while he went back to their car to use the police radio.

He picked up the mike, then rubbed it on his pants leg to remove the donut sugar. "This is car fifty-four. We've got a ten twenty-six here. I need a ten twenty-eight on a Mr. Nick Naught."

A voice came over the air from headquarters, heavily garbled. "What?"

"I said this is car fifty-four. We've got a ten twenty-six here. I need a ten twenty-eight on a Nick Naught."

"What?"

"I have a suspect in custody. I need vehicle registration information on a Nick Naught."

"Why didn't you say so?"

As Nick leaned against the car, he wondered if he knew anyone who would pull a practical joke like this, or if the police database really was that messed up.

Moments later the cop returned from the police car. "All right, you two. You can stand up straight. Goddamn database."

Nick and Annette glanced at each other and relaxed.

The cop wrote out a ticket and handed it to Nick along with his wallet.

"What's this?" Nick asked.

"A ticket. Your driver's license expired last week."

*　　*　　*

The library parking lot was mostly empty by the time Nick and

Annette parked and started walking toward the entrance.

"What a day," Nick said. He rubbed the back of his neck.

"It's been like this all day?"

"What a year."

Nick held back at the turnstile inside to let Annette go first. As she passed through the turnstile, it popped into the next rotation so quickly that it snapped her on the rear.

Annette looked back suspiciously, and Nick spread his hands in an "I'm innocent" gesture.

The reference section was as quiet as the parking lot. Nick looked for the computer books, while Annette took a detour to talk to a librarian.

Minutes later, Annette found Nick trying to decide what to look at first. She said, "Here's the list of the books he had checked out. What are we looking for?"

"I don't know," Nick said. "Dog-eared pages, underlining, whatever."

They opened book after book. Nick pulled an issue of *Mad Magazine* off the shelf, puzzled by its presence there, and put it back.

"Nick, look at this." Annette held a book, inside which were almost a dozen sheets of paper, each with apparently random sets of widely spaced letters on them.

Nick said, "Looks like a clue to me. But what do you make of it?"

"No idea."

A pronounced footfall sounded in the otherwise silent library.

"Let's get out of here," Nick said. "That can't be the cat."

On the way out, Nick again let Annette go first through the turnstile. This time, the turnstile operated normally, but Nick indulged an impulse and patted her on the rear.

Annette looked around quickly, and Nick spread his hands in

the "I'm innocent" gesture. He pointed at the turnstile.

Nick walked two more steps before he saw a turnstile reflection in a glass door, and he realized Annette must have been able to see him then. He slapped his palm against his forehead.

As they exited the library, Annette had a wry smile on her lips.

From the distance came the sound of a siren. Another noise, a softer sound, accompanied the siren, but it took Nick a second to realize where it was coming from. He grabbed Annette's hand and pulled her along, just as an incoming whistle increased in volume, and a baby grand piano crashed to the ground exactly where they had stood seconds earlier. Sheet music fluttered away in the breeze.

"Holy Scheherazade!" Nick said, looking at the rubble.

"Oh, my God!"

"You have any enemies in the L.A. Philharmonic?"

"No."

"Well, we missed death by piano by that much. Let's get out of here."

After they were safely in the car and a block away, Annette said, "No chance that was an accident?"

"Maybe with an upright, but a baby grand? No way."

★   ★   ★

Nick let Annette out next to her car in the restaurant parking lot. "I can follow you to wherever you're staying, just in case," he said. "Somehow they followed us there."

"I'm staying at the Red Moon Inn, but I'll be all right. You take care of yourself."

"Right. I'll call you tomorrow. And, Annette — you be careful, too. I don't want anything to happen to you."

Annette reached over and touched Nick's hand. Tenderly she said, "Me, neither."

★   ★   ★

As Nick watched her taillights recede, he sighed. He didn't turn to get into his car until the tiny red lights were lost in the smog.

Chapter 11

THE elevator in Nick's apartment building was silent except for a soft hiss of ventilation. Nick leaned against the wall and watched the floor indicator rise to his floor. The elevator stopped.

For a long moment the doors remained closed. The ventilation hiss seemed to increase in volume.

"You going to open the doors?" Nick asked finally.

The elevator's voice was ultra-calm. "I'm sorry, Dave. I'm afraid I can't do that."

Nick sighed. "Oh, come on, I'm tired."

The doors opened.

★   ★   ★

Nick entered his apartment, exhausted. He locked three separate locks on the inside of the door and pressed a button. A panel lit up, saying, "Alarm engaged."

On the living room wall was another large poster of a South Seas island. This one was twice as large as the poster in his bedroom.

Nick turned out the light and stumbled into the bedroom where he crashed onto the bed, clothes still on. It took him only moments to fall asleep.

Approximately an hour later, Nick was sleeping soundly, his breath a series of sighs. A door squeaked softly as it opened, then the sound of muted whispering filtered into the bedroom.

Suddenly a light flashed on, exposing Nick lying on the bed. While Nick was still groggy, a pair of hands grabbed and restrained him while another pair of hands sprayed an aerosol can in his face.

★   ★   ★

Nick's arms hurt, as he woke up uncomfortably. He couldn't see much because of the bright light hanging near his face, but he could see various instruments of torture against the dungeon walls.

He sat in a straight-backed chair, bound with thick ropes.

From the shadows, two business-suited men approached. Both had mean, pinched faces with dark eyes and dark stubble showing. Both wore white shirts.

The taller man said, "You have the right to remain silent —"

"Cut that nonsense," said the other. "You forget who we are?"

"Sorry."

"Mr. Naught, you've caused us a lot of trouble."

"Who the hell are you guys?" Nick demanded.

"We see thousands of people like you every year. You think you're so great, above it all. Well, you're not. And we're going to get what's coming to us, one way or another." The man showed what he had in his hands: a thumbscrew. The taller man brandished a whip.

"Get what?" Nick asked. "What have you got coming?"

"Sure, Mr. Naught. Pretend you don't know. We expected nothing less from you."

"Who the hell *are* you guys anyway? Just tell me what's going on."

"Oh, go on," said the taller one. "Tell him, Dan."

The other man pulled out his wallet and flipped it open to a badge. "We're the Internal Revenue Service, Mr. Naught. And we're going to get what you owe us, one way or another."

"The IRS? You've got to be kidding me."

"We *never* kid, Mr. Naught. About anything."

Nick looked at the ceiling. "Is this revolting, or what?"

The agents moved closer, menacingly.

Nick said, "Wait a minute. Wait a minute. How much do I owe you anyway?"

The taller man looked at his companion. "I don't know. I'd have to look it up."

"Well, do it. We've got all the time in the world."

The IRS agent moved to a computer terminal and punched a few keys. The video terminal made the mechanical sound a huge line printer would make as the screen scrolled.

"It says here on your return from four years ago you illegally rounded your office supplies deductions from $156.24 up to $157. Your check was therefore short by one dollar."

Nick was astonished. He said, "A dollar? One Goddamn dollar? I'll give you a Goddamn dollar. Let me get to my wallet. I'll give you a Goddamn *ten* dollars."

"Bad mistake, Mr. Naught. Never, ever, try to bribe an official of the IRS."

"I'm sorry. I lost my head. Just let me get to my wallet, and I'll give you the dollar. All right?"

The shorter agent asked his partner, "Is there anything in the rules about this?"

"No, I think it's permissible to pay a balance due amount in cash."

"Damn."

The taller agent smiled and said, "As long as you're here, would you care to contribute to the presidential campaign fund?"

★   ★   ★

The front door to Nick's apartment opened, and Nick was shoved through. He managed to catch his balance without falling on the floor, but he jammed one shin hard into the coffee table, and he winced.

The shorter IRS agent straightened his collar and said, "Just you watch your step, Mr. Naught. You miss another audit, and we'll be on your case. You bleeding-heart long-form scum make me sick."

Chapter 12

IN Nick's empty office, the phone rang. The phone answerer clicked on. "Nick Naught private investigations. Mr. Naught is sleeping late, so please leave a message."

Beep.

"Are you the Nick Naught who's the cousin of George Bauman? If you are, I've got a very large inheritance for you. Give me a call at 555-1212."

Just as the phone answerer clicked off, Nick entered the office. He pressed a button on the answerer.

"Sorry. No messages," it said.

Nick looked suspicious for a moment. Then he shook his head and said, "Nah."

He picked up the phone and dialed a very long number.

"Hey, Ron," he said when the call was answered. "Nick here. You still owe me a favor."

"Sure. Name it."

"There's a chance that someone's trying to cause a little trouble for me. Would you find out if Mike Johannson is still in the coop? He's the only person I can think of that holds a grudge."

"When do you want the answer?"

"Just leave a message if I'm not here. I've got an errand to run."

⋆   ⋆   ⋆

Nick waited in line while a bored woman license clerk waited on people ahead of him. He wondered which one of them owned the car out front that had bent over a parking meter.

When he finally reached the head of the line, he said, "I want to renew my license."

"All right. Let me just check this out." The blond clerk ran the license through a slot of the top of her terminal. As she looked at the screen, her dark eyes widened, and she made "tsk tsk" sounds. "It says here you had a moving violation last February."

"Yeah, I did, kind of. You see, I was chasing an escaped murderer."

"It also says here that in the eighth grade you dumped Rita Archibald."

Nick craned his neck to see the screen, but the clerk swiveled it so he couldn't.

She went on. "Since your license has expired, you're going to have to retake the test."

Nick sighed. "God. Not the test again."

★   ★   ★

Nick walked past a test taker standing at what looked like a voting booth with no privacy curtain. Jumper cables from the machine ran to bands on both of the test taker's wrists.

The machine asked, "Are parking lights used while your car is in motion?"

"Er — Yes."

Buzz! The test taker convulsed under the electrical shock.

The next station Nick passed was similar.

The machine asked, "Are you *always* supposed to use your turn signals when making turns or changing lanes?"

"Er — No."

Buzz! The test taker convulsed under the electrical shock.

At the third machine the test taker wore flowing robes and wore a pointed hat.

The machine asked, "At the present rate of population growth, by the year 2050 we will have only one square foot of land area per person. Does that make you want to reevaluate your stance on birth control?"

"Er — No."

Buzz! The test taker convulsed under the electrical shock.

★   ★   ★

Nick stood at a testing station with the jumper cables from the testing machine hanging from his wrists.

The machine asked, "What is the capitol of West Virginia?"

"Er — I don't know."

Buzz! Nick turned around casually to see if anyone was watching. The jumper cable on his right wrist hung from his shirtsleeve instead of from the strap on his wrist.

★   ★   ★

Nick sat before the camera. He brought up his hand to deal with an irresistible itch on his nose, and the flash went off.

"Next!" called the photographer before he laughed.

Chapter 13

BACK in his office, Nick pressed the button on the phone answerer.

"Two messages waiting." *Beep.*

The first caller said, "I saw that article about how you saved that old man who was about to get hit by a car. Well, that old man was my inheritance money. So now I'm stuck here that much longer. I think you stink."

Beep.

The second message was Nick's voice. "Ah, this is me. Just testing."

Nick raised his eyebrows, surprised that the messages got through.

The phone rang, and he picked it up. He opened his mouth as if to talk but didn't say anything. The phone answerer remained silent.

"Hello," he said finally.

"Nick, Ron. I just ran a check on Mike Johannson. He's still in Leavenworth, but he just has a couple of months left on his year. He was only in for those murders."

"Thanks for checking. I guess I must have been wrong."

"Sorry not to be more help. Now we're even, right?"

"Right. Thanks." Nick hung up.

The phone rang again. Nick picked it up, waited a second before saying, "Nick Naught."

"Hello. I'm calling from the air freight desk at the airport. We've got a package here for you to pick up."

"All right. I wasn't expecting anything, but I'll be out to get it."

Nick hung up, then picked up the phone and dialed a long number. "Can I speak to Annette Taylor?" he asked when the call completed. As he waited, he picked the clock out of the trash can. It still said 2:30 AM. He dropped it back in.

"Hello," Annette said.

"This is Nick. I think we need to get back together and — ah — get caught up on paperwork."

"I agree. What's a good time for you?"

"Maybe in a couple of hours. I've got to go out to the airport."

"Why don't I join you?"

"Fine. Pick you up in twenty minutes?"

"Okay."

Nick hung up. He started out of the office, but the phone rang again. He picked it up. "Nick Naught."

The phone answerer started up. "Nick Naught private —"

"I'm *on* the line," said Nick

"You don't have to be so testy," said the answerer.

"Mr. Naught, G. David Chamness here. You're a hard man to get hold of. I tried to get back to you yesterday, but the phone system just wouldn't cooperate."

"Yeah, I know what you mean. Say, could I put you on hold for just a moment?"

"Well, I suppose I would have to say that would be acceptable."

The auto-translator screen said, "Yes."

"Thanks," Nick said. He put the receiver back on the hook and walked out the door.

★　　★　　★

The airport was busy as Nick and Annette walked toward the entrance. The whine from a huge airliner taking off suddenly shifted in pitch and volume as it had to avoid a second plane.

Annette wore a tan skirt. Over her shoulder, hung a large purse on a long strap. "You okay?" she asked. "You seem a little tired."

"Yeah, I'm fine. I just had a nightmare last night."

Annette raised her eyebrows, but said nothing.

Near the doors was a newspaper vending machine.

"Yo! Wanna buy a paper?" it called.

Nick ignored it.

"Paper, man? Lady?"

Nick ignored it some more.

"Hey, I'm *talkin'* to you, mofo!"

Nick and Annette reached the sliding glass doors and found a middle-aged woman having trouble. She approached the open doors, and the doors promptly closed.

The woman backed up, and the doors opened.

She came closer. The doors closed.

The woman backed up. The doors opened.

Nick touched the woman's arm. "I think I've got this figured out. Can you stay here for just a moment?"

The woman nodded.

Nick took a running start and sped toward the gap between the doors. The doors started to close as they sensed him coming, but he managed to barely beat them as they pounded together hard enough to crush carbon into diamonds. As soon as he was through, they opened again.

Nick stayed far enough from the doors for them to stay open, and he gestured to Annette.

She imitated him, and got a running start. She sped through the doors safely, but this time when they pounded closed, they caught some material at the back of her skirt, and she was stuck.

Nick approached and saw what had happened. He gave a quick, hard pull on the material stuck in the door.

Rip.

"Sorry about that," Nick said.

As they walked away from the doors, Annette tried to see how much damage was done. Her skirt was missing a narrow vertical strip. Once they got far enough away, the doors opened once again.

Seconds later, the sudden sound of a horrendous crash reminded Nick about the older woman trying to get through. She screamed as Nick looked back and grimaced.

★   ★   ★

Occasionally as Nick and Annette walked, an airport P.A. system announcement sounded. Without exception the voices were all totally garbled.

They passed an attractive young woman of Japanese descent wearing a t-shirt that said, "Made in Japan," as a man on a motorized cart sped past fast enough for them to hear the Doppler shift.

They passed another newspaper vending machine, this one selling the *Bermuda Triangle Inquirer*. It gave a loud wolf whistle. Annette looked around, saw no one, but clutched the torn material at her back.

Nick said, "Just a minute. I've got an idea."

Moments later, he returned with an electric cart, and Annette joined him.

★   ★   ★

The air-freight counter had no one waiting in line.

"Here you are, sir," said the clerk. "Can I get you to sign for it?"

"Sure," Nick said.

The package was about the size of a paperback book, securely sealed with strong tape. Nick tried to open it, but his fingernails weren't sharp enough. He looked at the return address without recognizing it. He put the package in his jacket pocket and got back on the cart with Annette.

Threading through the crowd on the way back, they passed a woman who had set up a small table bearing the sign, "Citizens for Clean Books."

Nick swerved close enough to be heard and said, "So. Burned any good books lately?"

He heard no reaction from Annette, and he realized she had been fairly quiet for the past few minutes. He looked over at her questioningly.

Annette said, "You know, I must have thought about calling you a thousand times. Pretty masochistic, huh?"

Nick looked at the pedestrians ahead. "I wish you'd have called at least once. So I knew you were all right. I had to find out from Diana that you were still in town."

"Why should you care what happened to me? You deserted me."

They passed a teenage girl trying to get a drink from the water fountain. She pressed the button and water splattered all over her face. She gave it a second try, keeping her head clear. A jet of water flew twenty feet through the air and doused the newspaper being read by a seated man.

Nick frowned and said, "What the hell are you talking about?

You're the one who walked out on me."

"The hell I did! You walked out of the apartment that day and you didn't come back. I waited two weeks and decided you were never coming back so I moved in with Diana."

"I was in the hospital for Pete's sake! I called and left you five messages on the answering machine."

Annette looked uncertain. "You did? I never got them." More firmly she added, "Besides, I left *you* a bunch of messages on the answerer. You could have called me."

Nick said slowly, "I never got any messages. After all those fights I figured you'd had enough. I mean we had both threatened to move out, and I guess I decided your threats had actually been serious."

As they continued in silence, and Nick's stomach churned madly, they passed by the tattooed van driver, who smiled broadly when he saw Annette. The man began to run after Nick's cart, but changed his mind. He altered his course and raced toward an occupied cart, where he knocked the rider off, spilling the contents of the rider's shopping bag in a heap.

Nick and Annette passed a customer standing in front of a coffee machine. The cup didn't drop into the slot, so the coffee just flowed into the drain.

Annette finally said, "You really left mes —"

Nick started speaking simultaneously. "You didn't really walk —"

From behind them came a *yelp*, and Annette looked back. She saw the van driver on a cart that had just knocked over a kid. "Nick! Step on it! We're being followed by one of the guys who tried to kidnap me. If he has that knockout stuff they used on Ed —"

Nick looked back, then started to accelerate. Their cart sped faster, darting into holes that opened in the crowd.

The van driver followed in his cart, gaining because Nick's cart opened holes for both of the carts. The driver knocked a matronly lady sprawling. From a seated position, she turned, and, for someone who looked as refined as she did, gave the man a surprisingly rude gesture.

Suddenly, a man tall enough to be a formidable basketball player, riding another cart, appeared right in front of the van driver's cart, and the two carts crashed.

"Watch where you're going!" shouted the van driver.

"Why don't you?" said the jock. "I had the right of way!"

"And how do you figure that, toad face?"

Nick looked back and saw the confrontation interrupted by an approaching siren. The two cart drivers looked irritated when a third cart pulled up. This one sported red and blue flashing lights and was driven by a cart cop, a pot-bellied man wearing sunglasses and a hat. The cart logo said "L.A.X.P.D."

The cart cop got off his cart as the two drivers sat transfixed. The cart cop came over to the van driver's cart and rested one foot on the fender. "Looks like we've got a heap of trouble here, boys."

The jock said, "This idiot ran right into my side."

The van driver said, "Yeah, well, this idiot was going too fast."

The cart cop pulled out a pad of tickets and began to write. "Well, it looks like we got us a 'doin' ten in a five zone,' a 'drivin' without seat belts,' and a 'failure to yield right of way' just for starts. Lemme see your licenses." He hesitated. "You fellas insured for this?"

Nick circled the accident scene and came up behind the crashed carts. He drove slowly past the confrontation.

"That's the one who was driving the van," Annette said softly. "I'm absolutely certain of it."

Nick raised his voice and pointed to the van driver. "That's the guy, Officer. Back there a ways we passed a woman who was running to catch up with this guy. Apparently he was trying to molest her son in the restroom."

As Nick accelerated away, the van driver glared murderously, and the cart cop began to smile.

Nick and Annette were both silent in thought as they passed a newsstand where a man was reading a copy of *Digital Science Fiction*.

They rolled through the baggage claim area as the conveyer spewed pieces of luggage, most of which were smoking, falling open, and gashed.

The main doors were still malfunctioning when they got back. One door now had a big hole in the glass.

As they watched, a husky guy who looked like he played a lot of football tried the same trick Nick and Annette had used to get in. He ran, but he wasn't quite fast enough, and the doors clamped shut, catching him and trapping him between them. He dropped his bag, and it slid a couple of feet before it stopped.

As muscles stood out in cords on his arms, he pushed the doors slowly apart.

Nick said, "What do you want to bet his luggage is Sampsonite?"

As the man stood there, struggling against the pressure, obviously wanting to jump aside and let the doors snap shut, three people used the opportunity to get through the door. The last one turned around and took the beefy guy's wallet from his back pocket.

The guy lasted another couple of seconds, then jumped away and let the doors snap shut. He grabbed his luggage and began to run fast, obviously looking for another door out, so he could track down his wallet. The doors opened.

Nick looked at the doors a moment. Since no one else was near them, the doors stayed open. Nick walked over and pulled out the wall-plug. A second later, a guy in a jogging outfit raced through the open doors. The doors made no move to close. The jogger realized they hadn't reacted, and he moved slowly closer to investigate. He moved still closer to the doors, wary of being caught by them. As Nick and Annette moved past him, Nick touched the guy's arm, and the guy jumped.

Innocently Nick said, "What's the problem?"

Outside, the newspaper vending machine said, "Cheapskate!"

Nick hesitated, glanced around to see if anyone was looking, then pulled his gun and walked over to the vending machine.

"Er, nice day, isn't it?" said the machine.

Chapter 14

NICK and Annette rode without speaking for the first few minutes in the car. A light rain was falling, so the windshield wipers were on. The radio played rock music, and the wipers moved from side to side in perfect step with the music beat. The car hit a bump, and the station switched to classical. The wipers slowed down to match the tempo of the classical music. Annette banged the dash, and the station changed back to rock. The wipers sped up again to match the rock beat.

They drove past a parking lot with the sign in front, "Soon, a new office building on this spot. Your tax dollars at work."

A block later, they passed an office building with the sign in front, "Soon, a new parking lot on this spot. Your tax dollars at work."

Annette finally asked, "Have you ever seen the guy who was chasing us in the airport?"

"Nope. But if anyone else tries to follow us, I'll spot him."

Three car lengths behind, was a van following Nick's car. On the dash, a light blinked, as though the driver was tracking the car ahead. The van driver was Dennis Cotton, the red-nosed man who had nearly killed Nick in front of the hospital.

Nick and Annette passed through the rain, and the sun started coming out. They drove by a theater with the marquee sign saying, "Aliens 9 — In space no one can hear you vomit."

A police car flashed past, lights and siren on.

Nick took the package out of his coat pocket and handed it to Annette. "You got anything to open this with?"

"Maybe." Annette opened her purse and glanced through it. She looked back at the package and frowned. "What is it?"

"No idea."

The driver of the van behind them flipped open a compartment on the dash. He pressed a button. Numbers started to count down from thirty.

Annette said, "You get stuff you can't identify very often?"

"No. Not really. Why? Are you suggesting —"

"Maybe I'm just paranoid."

The numbers on the panel in the van kept counting down.

Nick said, "You know, this is starting to bother me a whole lot."

"It's about time."

The digits got down to five and suddenly started repeating. *Five. Five. Five...* The van driver noticed and pounded on the box.

Nick shouted, "Let's get rid of it!"

"Right!"

Nick tried to roll down his power window. Nothing happened. "It's stuck!"

Annette tried her window control. Nothing happened. "Mine, too!"

The van driver banged on the box again.

Nick and Annette simultaneously hit their car doors, and both windows started down. Nick threw the package up and out, arcing it into the road behind them.

The numbers on the van driver's box finally resumed their count. *Four. Three.*

"Finally!" the driver said. He looked back at the road, and was just realizing something lay on the pavement ahead when the numbers reached *One.*

He cried out and yanked the wheel as the counter reached *Zero*, and the small bomb exploded right under his van. Two tires instantly blew, and the back of the van nearly disintegrated. The driver lost control and crashed at the side of the road.

Nick watched in the rear-view mirror. "I've seen that van before. I'm sure of it."

"Let's get out of here," Annette said.

At Dennis's van, the smoke began to clear. Dennis struggled upright, opened the door, and fell out, mashing his already hurt shoulder. "I hate this Goddamn job!"

At the sound of an approaching siren, Dennis looked hopeful. The ambulance pulled even with his van, without slowing down, and sped away, going wherever it was already going.

Annette frowned. "That bomb was meant for us, you realize that?"

"I sure do." Nick turned a corner. "You might even say it had my name on it."

"I'm not joking! Someone just tried to kill us."

"Not to mention me," said the car.

They passed a huge building with an animated sign saying, "Hackers' Military Secrets."

Nick hesitated. "I'm sorry. I guess I'm a little punchy and confused. It's like whoever's after you is psychotic. One time they try to kidnap you, the next time they try to kill. And that package could easily have just gotten me without hurting you."

"Well, what do we do?"

A police car flashed past, siren on.

"Well, we could call the police."

They passed a stalled car with its hood open. A man in a business suit was bent over the engine compartment, working on it. A black, ugly part of the engine flew out of the engine compartment and bounced on the ground several yards away.

Annette shook her head. "We should live so long. That desert island of yours is looking better and better all the time."

Nick checked the rear-view mirror. "First things first. We've got to work fast and get this figured out. And I've got an idea."

Chapter 15

NICK and Annette pulled up in front of KSMY in Nick's car. Nick squeezed into a parking space and killed the engine.

The car said, "Can I come, too?"

Nick raised his eyebrows. "Wait here, will you? You can listen to the radio."

While Nick and Annette waited in the lobby, Connie and Howard were live on the TV monitor. Howard moved to a new story. "In a bizarre shoot out at the Beverly Hilton this morning, the last surviving Blood and the last surviving Crip killed each other."

Connie took her turn. "On a bitter note, four young moviegoers were gunned down in a multiplex theater last night. Larry Costa is in custody after a group of survivors kept him at bay for six hours until the police arrived. The feature was last year's remake of *Old Yeller*. Allegedly, at an intensely emotional and very quiet point in the film, the four victims' hourly watch chimes went off."

A door opened and Earle Thompson came in. "Sorry to keep you waiting. Come on in."

"Thanks," Nick said.

Nick introduced Annette as they walked down the hall. They passed Curtis's closed office door, and Nick could hear the buzzer.

At the end of the corridor, Earle pointed into a room off the hallway. "There you are. Help yourselves."

Nick thanked him, and Earle went back to work.

The small room contained two photocopiers. On the wall was a framed photocopy labeled, "Posterior of the Month."

Nick turned to Annette. "Let's see those papers."

She got the stack of papers from her purse and handed the sheets to him.

Nick put an original on the glass of the first copier. "One copy."

The copier said, "Okay." Light flashed, the mechanism whirred, and a totally blank page fell into the hopper.

"Darker," Nick said. "One copy."

"Okay." The copier worked and a totally black page came out.

Nick frowned. "You got anything in between?"

The copier flashed, and a half-white, half-black page came out.

Nick sighed. He pulled up the cover to get the original back, but the paper was gone. "Where the hell's my paper?" Nick kicked the machine, and it spit out the original.

"Can't take a joke, huh?" the copier said.

Nick shook his head, moved to the second copier, and put in the original. "One copy."

The copier mechanism did nothing, but it said, "Take a hike. I saw what you did to Tommy."

Nick hesitated. "I'm going to count to three. If you're not running by then, I'm going to take —" He glanced at the first copier. "Tommy — apart piece by piece. And then I'm going to replace him with a different model."

After a short silence the copier said, "*What* model?"

Instantly the first copier said, "Dickie, you jerk!"

"Just kidding," said the second copier. Its light flashed, the mechanism whirred, and a good copy came out.

"That's more like it," Nick said. He fed the copy back into the blank paper tray and put the second original on the glass. "One copy."

The copier worked properly again. The ejected copy looked denser because it had letters from both pages on it. Nick again put the copy in the blank paper bin and inserted the third original. The next copy contained partial words. Moments later, the final cycle completed and a full-looking page of text came out.

Nick and Annette examined the completed text.

Nick frowned. "I don't understand. This makes it seem like Ed's been using a computer virus to steal from someone."

"Ed wouldn't do anything like that. There's got to be some mistake."

"Maybe we should go back to the house and look at his computer more closely."

Annette shrugged.

On their way out, they again passed the closed door to Jim Curtis's office, and the buzzer was still going.

Nick stopped, glanced around, and kicked the door once with the side of his shoe. The buzzer stopped. Nick grinned.

Annette had stopped when Nick did. She looked puzzled, but Nick was already moving again.

Outside, a "while you were out" note stuck under Nick's windshield wiper fluttered in the breeze.

Nick read the note aloud. "We've got Ed Taylor. If you want to talk to him, be at Knowlton's Repair Works at ten tonight." He glanced around but saw no one who looked like an obvious candidate for having left the note.

"Nick, that sounds like a trap," Annette said as they got into the car. She had to raise her voice until Nick turned down the volume on the radio.

"Sure it does. I watch movies, too. But *they* are going to be there, whoever they are. This might be the only way to find out what's going on."

As Nick pulled out into the street, they passed a man taking a sledgehammer to his car.

Annette looked over at Nick and said resolutely, "Well, Ed's my brother, so I'm going, too."

"No way. It would be too dangerous."

The car said, "Oh, come on, Nick. What's the harm?"

Chapter 16

NICK's car cruised slowly down the dark, rain-slick street as the windshield wiper kept clearing the drizzle. The neighborhood did not look affluent. Warehouses with broken windows lined the street, and half of the streetlights were burned out.

Nick pointed. "Isn't that it over there?"

A flash of lightning illuminated the dark street and the sign, "Knowlton's Repair Works." Thunder echoed.

"Yeah," Annette said. "It looks creepy."

"We're early, but I'd better go in now anyway." Lightning flashed, and loud thunder sounded.

"Well, creepy or not, I'm coming."

"I still think you should wait in the car." Just as Nick spoke, lightning flashed, and thunder crashed again.

"Not on your life," said Annette.

"It's *your* life I'm —" As he spoke, lightning flashed, and

ALL FOR NAUGHT   79

thunder boomed again, and Nick realized the same thing had happened the last several times he spoke. "What a coincidence —" More
lightning and thunder.

Nick said, "Every time I say something —" More lightning and
thunder.

"Hey, this is fun." More lightning and thunder.

Annette and the car spoke simultaneously. "Men!"

Chapter 17

NICK and Annette dashed across the dark street in the rain, amid the
thunder and lightning, trying to avoid the deepest oily puddles.

The door squeaked loudly as they entered the warehouse. The
interior was poorly lit by naked light bulbs that revealed a freight elevator ahead of them. Old packing boxes filled to overflowing with
trash littered the room.

They walked forward cautiously, seeing no one. Grit crunched
beneath their shoes. Nick could smell dust. They followed a path
through the boxes that lead toward the elevator. Stuck to the elevator
cage was a note, which Nick grabbed. "All it says is 'fourth floor,'" he
whispered.

Annette whispered back, "The idea of going up in that thing
makes me nervous."

"Me, too. That's what they'll be expecting." Through the walls,
thunder rumbled. Nick whispered to the freight elevator, "Go to the
fourth floor."

"You talkin' to me?" The voice used for the elevator had a Bronx
accent.

"Shhh. Yes."

"What?"

Nick slapped his palm against his forehead. "Go to the fourth floor."

"By myself?" asked the elevator.

"Yes."

"Why should I do that?"

"Because I told you to. Because of the second law of robotics."

"Say what?"

"Just do it, will you?"

"Gimme ten bucks?"

"What?"

Suddenly Annette said softly but emphatically, "Go up to the fourth floor, or I'll cut your cable off."

Silently the elevator started to rise.

Nick looked at Annette incredulously.

"I used to have a temperamental microwave," she said.

Nick shook his head. "We'd better find the stairs."

They saw two stairwells each about thirty yards away on opposite sides of the building. Nick pointed to one and they walked as softly as they could toward it. The one Nick chose was even darker than the room they had walked through. Nick drew his gun as he led the way up the dark stairwell. "Shhh."

Only two seconds later, Nick stepped on a squeaky dog's toy. They both jumped. Nick's heart began to slow down, and he picked up the toy.

"Great work," said Annette. "Do you think they have a dog?"

"Pets in a place like this?" Nick tossed the toy away and moved up a step. A cat cried loudly, and something moved under Nick's foot. From the darkness came a diminishing *pitter-patter* sound.

Annette said dryly, "Maybe we should split up."

"Very funny. Now be quiet."

★   ★   ★

Upstairs on the fourth floor, near the freight elevator shaft, Jerry Pershing and Skid Peck, the two musclemen who had been following Annette, waited impatiently. The elevator approached. The two men drew their guns, and Skid glanced at his digital watch. Beyond them sat Ed Taylor, bound in a chair, tape across his mouth.

The elevator arrived, empty.

"What the hell's going on?" Jerry asked.

"You talkin' to me?" said the elevator.

"Shut up," Jerry said.

Skid said, "Where are they?"

"You talkin' to me?" said the elevator.

"Shut up," Skid said.

Jerry took a deep breath. "All right. No need to panic." He pushed a switch on a small box.

Around the warehouse, a series of locks clicked closed and bolts slid home, securing the building.

"Okay," Jerry said. "No one's going anywhere." He pushed another switch on the box.

On the first floor, Gizmo, a small robot that looked a lot like a canister vacuum cleaner with a gun muzzle added came to life downstairs. Gizmo rolled forward silently.

Jerry said, "Gizmo should be on duty now. You go downstairs. I'll wait here."

★   ★   ★

On the first floor, Gizmo rolled through a darkened area of the room. The cat cried out again.

Gizmo instantly swiveled, and the gun muzzle tilted down, scanning, searching. "Damn cat." Gizmo's voice had been cloned from a macho action-film star, resonant bass, with a noticeable accent. Presumably, the designers felt the voice was compelling in those situations where no one could see Gizmo. When Gizmo *was* in sight, the voice gave the impression that a ventriloquist must have been part of the team.

★   ★   ★

Upstairs, Skid swung the elevator gate aside, got in, and swung it closed again. "First floor," he said.

"First floor *what?*" the elevator said.

Skid hit himself on the forehead. "First floor, *please.*"

The elevator suddenly dropped about two feet. Skid panicked, then caught himself as he realized he was no longer falling.

The elevator said, "Just kidding."

★   ★   ★

Nick and Annette crept up the stairs and reached the second floor. They stayed closed together and spoke in ultra-soft whispers.

Nick said, "Let's stay on this floor for a few minutes. By now they've seen the elevator. It's easier if they're looking for us than if we're looking for them."

"Okay by me," said Annette.

They walked along a wide corridor with darkened rooms off each side. They hadn't gone two meters when they passed a full-length mirror. Annette jumped at the moving reflection, then relaxed. Not far from the mirror, was a faded "Rambo 8" poster showing an *old* Stallone with an automatic rifle. Below the poster a sign said, "The wars in Argentina, Brazil, Cuba, Denmark, Egypt, and elsewhere need a few good men."

★   ★   ★

Little levers extended from Gizmo's body, and he started climbing the stairs. "Damn stairs."

★   ★   ★

Nick and Annette continued down the corridor, turning occasionally as it made turns around odd-sized rooms. They came to a corner and hesitated, not able to see if anyone might be waiting around the bend. Nick readied his gun and popped around the corner, but no one was there. They kept walking.

Halfway down the hall sat a trio of soft drink machines, two Coca Colas and a Pepsi.

"Thirsty?" Nick asked, joking.

Annette shook her head, but the Pepsi machine responded.

"A drink sure would hit the spot right now. What is life without Pepsi?" said the Pepsi machine, its voice cloned from an I-don't-get-no-respect comedian.

One of the Coca Cola machines said, "Get real. Be Real. Don't touch that inferior stuff, hoser, eh?"

The second Coca Cola machine said, "Yeah. I mean really, eh? Beauty."

"Well at least *talk* to me," the Pepsi machine pleaded. "I'm bored as hell, and these two dorks won't even talk to me."

Nick and Annette shook their heads in wonderment. They moved on.

"Wait! Don't go. I'll give you a free Pepsi. I'll give you both a free Pepsi."

★ ★ ★

Gizmo reached the second floor. "Phew!" He rolled down the corridor, following Nick and Annette.

Gizmo reached the Rambo poster. Instantly he swiveled and pointed the muzzle toward the poster. "You've got ten seconds to put down the gun."

Gizmo's gun muzzle took aim on Rambo's chest.

Silence.

"You've got five seconds to put down the gun."

Silence.

Time ran out. Gizmo fired at the poster. The wall exploded and crashed down.

The cat cried out, and the *pitter-patter* of running feet sounded in the darkness.

Gizmo swiveled and fired at where he thought the cat sounds had come from. The firing was like machine gun fire. "Damn cat."

★   ★   ★

Nick and Annette neared another stairwell.

"What was that?" Annette asked.

"I don't want to know. Let's go up another floor."

★   ★   ★

The collapsed wall had torn a hole in the corridor floor, so Gizmo couldn't get past. He swiveled, examined the situation for a moment, and then retreated. "I'll be back."

★   ★   ★

Skid got out of the elevator. He scanned the surroundings for signs of Nick and Annette, and saw nothing.

He walked toward the stairwell.

★   ★   ★

Nick and Annette reached the third floor, and they started along the corridor.

From ahead of them came a constant murmuring, like the distant sound of a giant cocktail party.

They moved along the corridor and cautiously approached the door to a very large room. They peeked around the corner. Inside was an enormous collection of appliances including washer/dryers, televisions, old vending machines, phone answerers and other electronic equipment. They were all talking to each other. About the only word heard clearly was a frequent "What?"

Nick said, "If you know me when I'm old, don't ever send me to a rest home."

"You should live so long."

They continued along the corridor. Suddenly Gizmo was visible in the distance.

"What's that ahead?" Nick asked.

"No idea. Unless it's vacuuming."

As Gizmo approached, Nick and Annette ducked into a room to hide.

Gizmo went by the door to the room, continuing on toward the noises down the hall. Nick gestured toward the direction Gizmo had come from.

They tiptoed into the hallway and started their getaway. They had almost reached the stairwell, when Gizmo's voice sounded loudly. "You've got ten seconds to put down the gun."

Nick and Annette turned slowly to face Gizmo, who was now very close. Suddenly Nick grabbed Annette's hand and pulled her toward the stairwell.

They hit the stairwell just as Gizmo said, "You've got five seconds to put down the gun."

Gizmo saw them vanish into the stairwell. "Crap."

Gizmo rolled to the stairs in time to hear the pair's downward footsteps echoing. "Damn stairs."

Nick and Annette dashed out of the stairwell onto the second floor, running as quietly as they could. They passed the mirror again and reached the hole in the hallway floor.

"Come on," Nick said. He made a running start and jumped over the hole. He gestured to Annette to follow.

She hesitated, looking down into the darkness. Finally she got a firm grip on the large purse, and she jumped, too. Her feet skidded on the floor for an instant before Nick steadied her.

Nick looked back at the corridor and narrowed his gaze. "Just a minute."

He jumped back over the hole. Not knowing how much time they had, he raced to the mirror on the wall, struggled briefly, and yanked it free.

Near the edge of the hole, he knelt and positioned the mirror lengthwise on the floor, diagonally across the hallway just in front of the hole. He angled it so Gizmo would see neither the hole nor his own reflection as he approached.

Satisfied with his handiwork, Nick backed up for another running start. He jumped over the mirror and just cleared the hole. He teetered on the edge for a second before Annette yanked him forward.

Nick felt her hand on his wrist, and he felt like he'd just almost lost her again. Or vice versa. He said softly, "Damn that answering machine anyway."

Annette reached up and touched his cheek. Her eyes looked larger than normal. Nick's cheek tingled.

The mood was suddenly broken as Gizmo rolled quickly along the hallway. They ran a few yards and stopped just around a corner, looking back at Gizmo.

Gizmo sensors twitched, and he said very quickly, "You've got one second to put down the gun!"

Nick called out, "Get serious!"

Gizmo raced forward, firing at the same time. From their position, ducked behind the corner, Nick and Annette could hear Gizmo as he crashed through the mirror and fell into the hole. As he dropped, Gizmo said, "Damn hole!"

Chapter 18

GUN in hand, Skid moved quietly along the corridor and cautiously approached a corner he couldn't see around. A floorboard creaked somewhere in front of him, and he became even more cautious. The very next floorboard he stepped on squeaked.

Nick and Annette crept along the same corridor, moving toward the same corner. They, too, heard a noise ahead.

"Quiet!" Annette whispered.

As they approached the blind corner from the side opposite Skid, they moved even more quietly.

They crept closer and closer to the corner. Nick was trying to decide whether to stick his head around the bend, when the sound of Skid's digital watch chime came from just around the corner.

Nick grinned. Quickly he grabbed Annette's purse, held it by the top of the long strap, and whipped it as hard as he could around the corner. The purse clunked loudly as it connected with Skid.

Nick stepped around the corner. Skid was sagging. His gun fell from his hand. Nick caught him as he started to fall to the floor. To Annette he said, "Help me with this guy."

Annette helped him drag Skid's unconscious body into a nearby room. Using the man's shirt and pants for bindings, they muffled his mouth and made sure he wasn't going anywhere anytime soon. And now Annette had a gun, too.

As they finished, Nick said, "This isn't the guy we saw before. He must still be in here somewhere."

"Upstairs?"

"Let's go. If your brother really is in the building, that's probably where."

Nick and Annette stealthily went to the end of the corridor and crept up the stairs. Now and then Annette's purse made soft tinkling sounds.

They reached the fourth floor without encountering anyone else and started creeping down the corridor.

They slowly approached the elevator shaft. The elevator was there, but it was empty.

They moved a little farther down the corridor, and encountered a brightly lit room. Against the back wall, still roped into his chair, sat Ed Taylor.

Annette cried "Ed!" and ran toward his chair, using no caution.

"Shhh," Nick said, following quickly, surveying as he went. One wall of the room was broken by a small hallway leading to another room. Nick tried to keep watch on the small hallway and the way they had come.

Annette had started to take the tape off Ed's mouth, but Nick grabbed her arm. "I don't like this."

Annette hesitated. Nick could see she was worried, but that she was also concerned about how Ed was. Ed was not reacting to their presence.

Nick suddenly glanced back down the small corridor, unsure if he had heard some noise from there or not.

In a room at the other end of the short corridor, Jerry Pershing pressed a button on a hockey-puck-sized device. An inset display flipped to ten and started counting down. Satisfied, Jerry slid the device down the hall.

A half-second later, Nick saw the canister sliding toward him and Annette. "Let's get out of here!"

Nick grabbed the chair Ed was tied to and started pulling him out of the room. Too slow. The combination was so heavy and awkward, it was hernia time.

Annette saw the canister approaching. She swung her purse off her shoulder and, holding the strap, easily batted the canister back the way it had come.

On seeing Nick's astonished expression, she said, "I used to play hockey."

Jerry saw the canister reverse its path. "Damn it! I hate this God-damn job!"

Nick and Annette stood petrified, watching the canister slide back to the room it had come from. A second passed.

Poof! The canister exploded, releasing an enormous cloud of dense smoke.

In a nasal tone, like in the old Roadrunner cartoons, Nick said, "Beep beep."

Nick and Annette moved down the corridor cautiously as the smoke began to thin.

Wisps of smoke still lingered in the air when they found Jerry sprawled on the floor, unconscious.

Nick said, "Now *this* guy we recognize."

"The guy from the airport. Now we can find out who he is."

Jerry had a computer diskette and a pencil in his shirt pocket. Nick took the disk and rolled Jerry's body over to expose his wallet, which he also took. Nick flipped through the wallet, and he began to frown. "Oh oh. This is not really good news. This says his name is Jerry Pershing. And he works for Major Opportunity Business."

"We've been fighting a company? That doesn't make any sense."

Nick started back toward Ed's chair. "Not just any company. M.O.B. is to business what a switch-blade is to a letter opener."

Annette grimaced. "Let's get Ed and get out of here. Or do you think there might be more of them around?"

"I don't know. Maybe Ed knows."

Ed stared just as blankly as he had before.

Annette slapped him lightly. "Ed. Ed. Wake up."

Nick began to untie Ed. "I don't think it's any use. He's comatose."

Moments later they again moved forward cautiously. Nick staggered beside Annette as he carried Ed. Ed was *heavy*.

Annette whispered, "Take the elevator?"

"Thanks anyway. I've already had enough abuse today."

They reached the stairwell unchallenged. Nick pulled his gun as he tried to keep Ed balanced. "Cover the rear, and be careful," he whispered.

"Right." Annette pointed her gun back down the corridor.

Nick stepped into the darkened stairwell. He took a couple of steps down. Suddenly the cat cried out, and something moved under Nick's foot. He lurched forward into the darkness. The next step wasn't where it should be, and Nick tipped forward, Ed's weight now moving fast enough that Nick passed the point of no return. He and Ed fell down nearly the whole flight of stairs.

Annette scrambled down the stairs, rushing to catch up with them. At the next floor landing, Ed and Nick lay in a heap.

Nick picked himself up, found his gun, and assumed a stealthy posture, gun extended. He took a couple of steps forward, listening intently. He called out softly, "Here, kitty, kitty, kitty."

"Stop that!" said Annette.

Nick looked sheepish. "Just kidding," he said unconvincingly.

★   ★   ★

Nick carried Ed as he and Annette crept across the floor toward the front door. They passed Gizmo, who lay flat on his head, surrounded by rubble from the hole in the ceiling. The wheels and levers on his base couldn't help him right himself.

As they watched, a dog approached Gizmo and started to sniff. Gizmo yelled, "Get away! Get away from me! You've got one second to put down that leg."

Nick and Annette left Gizmo where he was and moved toward the front door. Annette tried the door. "It's locked," she said.

Nick shifted his weight and aimed a solid kick at the door. The door, together with the doorframe, fell slowly outward and crashed onto the ground, spreading a cloud of dust into the night air. "No problem."

Annette led the way. As Nick walked through the doorway, he

clunked Ed's head hard against the wall.

Annette turned quickly. "What was that? Did Ed say something?"

Nick looked down at Ed's head and said, "I really doubt it."

Chapter 19

"ED! Are you all right?" Annette asked. She and Nick sat in front seat of the car.

Ed sat the back seat and groaned. "What's going on?"

"You tell us," Nick said. "We just got you back from a couple of M.O.B. guys."

Ed put both hands to his head.

Nick didn't feel he should interrupt to explain the bruise.

Ed said. "Oh yeah. Boy, those people were angry. I —" He hesitated. "I found out that M.O.B. made a computer virus. It's been siphoning off money from everywhere. Anyway, I managed to break into their computer system and get their passwords. I had just finished modifying the virus to reverse it — to take money out of M.O.B. Somehow they must have tracked me down, and they grabbed me." He patted his pockets. "Damn. I had it on a diskette, but they must have it now."

"A diskette like this?" Nick asked, showing what he had taken from Jerry.

"Yeah. That's it!" Ed said. "All I need to do is run it on their computer, and it'll reverse the damage."

"But why did they try to get Annette?" Nick asked.

Ed looked at Annette. "I was using a borrowed disk with your name on it. They wouldn't believe me when I told them you had nothing to do with this."

"What now?" Annette asked.

Nick started the car. "Now we find a phone booth and do some bargaining with M.O.B. Or try. This'll probably be like taking candy from a pit bull."

★   ★   ★

Nick stood impatiently at the phone booth as his call connected.

"Major Opportunity Business," said the voice on the phone.

Nick took a deep breath. "One of your people has been trying to kill me. His name is Jerry Pershing. You'd better call off anyone else who's after me, or you'll never see him and his partner again."

"And who am I speaking to, please?" The voice was bored, as though Nick had just asked for the time.

"Nick Naught. I'm a private detective."

"Please stand by, while I get more information."

"All right. But hurry."

Annette called out from the car, "What's happening?"

"He's getting more information. At M.O.B., they're probably up to their buns in it." Nick fidgeted as he waited. He looked at his watch.

A moment later he looked at his watch again. "What's the holdup?"

"Please just stand by," said the voice. "I'll have the information in just a minute."

Nick was growing suspicious and nervous. "No. Let's talk now."

"It will be just another minute, sir."

"All right. But hurry." Nick dropped the receiver so it

hung from the cord. He ran to the car.

Nick got in and started the car. As he pulled away from the curb, he said, "I don't like this. I bet they're figuring out where this number is. I'll have to call them back from someplace else."

They had traveled less than a third of a block when the phone booth Nick had just left exploded in a luminous orange ball of flame.

Nick looked at the red and yellow destruction, and said under his breath, "Hold all my calls."

A police car flashed past, siren on, without slowing down.

"That's incredible," said Annette. "What are we up against?"

"I don't know. This is even worse than breaking up the phone company." Nick had another thought. "I'm glad I didn't call from home."

★   ★   ★

Nick retrieved a stack of coins from his pocket. When he had deposited enough of them, the phone played video game winning sounds. Nick dialed a *long* number.

"Thank you for using AT&T," said a voice. "The charge will be $10.00 for the first three minutes."

"If you use Sprint," said another, "the charge will be only $9.50."

"If you use MCI, the charge will be only $9.40."

"AT&T here. Did I say $10.00? I meant $9.35."

"Sprint will do it for $9.00."

One of the other voices softly said, "Slut."

"MCI $8.90."

Nick asked, "Do I hear $8.85?"

"AT&T here. $8.87. That's our final offer."

"Going once. Twice. Three times. *Now* will you put me through?"

"Very well, sir," said the AT&T voice. "For each additional minute that will be $20."

The phone began to ring at the other end. When it was answered, a voice said, "McCormick residence."

Nick said, "I need to talk to Mr. McCormick. This is a major emergency."

"I'm very sorry, sir. It's past Mr. McCormick's bedtime."

"Didn't you hear me? I said this is an emergency."

"I heard you, sir. Maybe if you call back next Wednesday he'll have more time."

"I'm not making myself clear. I'm —"

Click. The connection was broken.

"Damn it. I didn't even get my $8.87 worth." Nick flipped open the coin return. There was nothing there. He banged the phone, and it made a rude noise.

Chapter 20

NICK and Annette and Ed drove along a dark street. Ed was still a slow conversationalist.

"That's it. We're doomed," said Nick.

Annette turned in her seat. "We can't just give up now. We got Ed back. They can't just kill us."

"No? What happened to that phone booth? Sorry, wrong number?"

"But we can't quit now. Not while they could find us any time. And it won't help to retreat to your island. They'd find us there just as easily."

"'Us?'"

"'Us' if you and I are still alive."

Nick glanced over at her and even in the darkness could see her gaze on him. He drove in silence for half a block, thinking about how much he had missed her, then suddenly made a hard right turn. "Call me crazy, but I think it's time we paid a personal visit to Mr. McCormick. Just as soon as we make a stop or two. Is that an autoteller ahead? We could use some money."

It was indeed an autoteller. A minute later Nick entered the brightly lit chamber. Annette and Ed waited in the car.

Nick fed his card into the slot. "I need five hundred cash."

The autoteller sounded like an old traveler's check advertiser. "Very well, sir. Please enter your personal code letters."

Nick entered the letters on a small keyboard.

"I'm sorry, but your account has a balance of only two hundred and fifty dollars."

Nick hesitated. "Look, I'm going to toss a coin. If you call it correctly, I'll give you five hundred. If you're wrong, you give me the extra two fifty. How about those odds?"

"Well — all right."

Nick flipped a coin and held it against the back of his hand. "All right. Call it."

"Heads," said the autoteller.

Nick rolled his hand forward, so he showed the machine the coin tails up on his palm, instead of heads up on the back of his hand. "Tails. Sorry, you lose."

"Crap! Okay. Here you are." The drawer opened, and Nick took out the $500.

"Thanks. But look, I can't take your money like this. Just to show I'm a good sport, I'm going to even things up. I have another account here, under my pen name. I'm a writer. You have a record of that account? For Jerry Pershing?"

"Yes."

"Fine. Just transfer two fifty over to cover this."

There was a short delay. "Completed. Thank you, sir! That leaves six hundred and forty-two thousand in your Pershing account."

Nick tried to conceal a sudden grin. He glanced around, then turned back to the autoteller camera lens. "You know, I just realized. I've got a tax payment coming up. Would you go ahead and transfer over the whole account?"

After another short delay, the autoteller said, "Certainly, sir. All finished. Anything else?"

"No, thanks. Maybe tomorrow."

★   ★   ★

"You sure seem happy," Annette said when Nick got back into the car.

"Sometimes I just love my job," Nick said. "Maybe it's the danger."

★   ★   ★

In a department store, Nick and Annette walked down an aisle.

"What exactly are we looking for?" she asked.

"I'll know when I see it. Something to make it easier to get in without attracting a lot of attention."

"Something like this?" Annette pointed to a large box on the shelf. It was labeled, "Acme All-Purpose Break-In Kit."

"Yeah! That's terrific. And this is even better." Nick pointed next to it, at a similar package, but larger, labeled, "Acme All-Purpose Break-In Kit. Economy size. Enough for two people."

The sales clerk who rang up the sale wore a name tag saying, "N. KNOTT." His mustache looked as if it had been scribbled above his upper lip.

Chapter 21

NICK's car was parked beside a tall stone fence. In the weak light spilling from the interior of the car, Nick and Annette finished pulling stuff out of the break-in kit and loading it into small pockets in the multi-pocket hunters' vests they now wore.

A sign on the fence said, "No trespassing, no stopping, no loitering, no kidding."

Nick leaned into the car and said, "How about if you stay here, Ed? You've had enough for one day."

Ed nodded, then rubbed the bruise on his head. Nick grimaced.

Annette put the gun they had confiscated in the warehouse in the back seat with Ed. "You probably need this more than I do," she said. Ed nodded and left the gun where it was.

Nick pulled out an ugly gun designed for shooting a grappling hook attached to a rope.

Annette said, "This is crazy, you know."

"You said that already." Nick readied the gun. "I always wanted to do this."

He aimed for the top of the fence and pulled the trigger. Instead of shooting the grappling hook up just a few yards, the grapple shot up like a rocket, as if it were trying to reach the top of Mount Everest. Rope kept coming and coming out of the supply reel.

Annette said, "Maybe this is the high-rise kit."

Nick pulled on the cord to draw it tight. He drew and drew and drew.

★   ★   ★

Inside the fence, Nick and Annette sneaked from tree to tree in the moonlight. Ahead an M.O.B. guard paced near a pool of light spreading from a flood lamp mounted on the building wall.

"What do we do now?" Annette asked. "Do I try to seduce him?"

"Don't be silly."

"What exactly do you mean by that?" Annette looked frostily at him.

"Nothing. Nothing. I just mean it's not appropriate just now. Maybe later." Nick winked at her and wiggled his eyebrows. "I've got the tranquilizer dart gun. I'll shoot him. Simple."

"You got a *small* tranquilizer dart to shoot *me* with?"

Nick took aim and shot the guard.

The guard twitched, then apparently decided he had just gotten bit by a mosquito. A long second passed. Finally in mid-step the guard keeled over.

Nick and Annette started forward. Suddenly Nick stopped.

"What's wrong?" Annette asked.

Nick lifted the heel of his shoe to examine it. "They must have a dog."

A half-minute later, they passed a large electronic bug zapper. Underneath it, on a pile of dead insects, lay several dead squirrels and birds.

Nick stopped suddenly. "You see that?" he asked, pointing.

In the distance, a security camera panned back and forth.

"Yeah," she said. "Maybe the paint gun would work here?"

"Sounds good. How's your aim."

"We'll see."

Annette aimed her gun, held her breath, and gently squeezed the trigger. A blossom of black paint formed on the camera lens. Not even trying to contain her satisfaction, Annette blew across the gun muzzle.

In the monitoring room inside the house, two M.O.B. guards were leaning back in chairs, paying more attention to their card game than to the bank of video monitors. A monitor showing an expanse of grass and trees in the yard suddenly went dark.

"Not another one," said one of the guards.

In the vast bank of video monitors, about half of them no longer worked.

"Where's the trouble log?" asked the other guard. "I'll make a note of it." A huge volume, the size of the Braille edition of the New York state phone book, crashed onto the desk in front of him.

Nick and Annette worked their way closer to the building.

"So far so good," Annette said. "Where do we go next?"

"This may tell us." Nick used a flashlight to illuminate a map on the wall. One label said, "You are here." One of the doors was labeled, "West entrance." The keypad adjacent to the door looked like a touch-tone phone pad.

Nick looked at his notes, then typed in a number, and the door lock *clicked*. "Thank you, Ed," he said softly.

They opened the door and moved slowly through, into the building. Annette touched Nick's arm and pointed.

Down the hall was another monitoring camera panning slowly toward their location. Annette aimed her paint gun and shot at it.

Another monitor went dark.

They walked stealthily down the hall. At the next corner they peered around and saw another guard approaching a coffee vending machine. "Coffee, black," the guard said. He sounded bored and half asleep.

The machine dropped a cup into the front slot, and then squirted the man with coffee. The coffee did the trick; he was awake instantly. He kicked the machine.

As if the machine was retaliating, it squirted him again.

The guard's face turned mean. He carefully moved to one side of the machine and gave it a good hard kick.

The machine changed its aim and squirted him again.

The guard pulled out his gun. "That's it! That's the last bugging time!"

Nick reached around the corner and shot the guard with a tranquilizer dart. The guard keeled over.

Nick and Annette moved around the corner. They dragged the guard over to a door and stuffed his body into a closet with an automatic vacuuming machine that looked uncomfortably like Gizmo.

They continued along the corridor, until stopping at an elevator next to another you-are-here map. Beside the map was a sign that said, "The price of freedom is eternal vigilance."

Nick looked long and hard at the elevator button. As he was about to push it, Annette grabbed his hand.

"Look." She pointed to a sign saying, "Stairs."

"Excellent idea."

At the next level up, they peeked through the doorway crack and saw no one.

They moved along a carpeted corridor and came to a closed door bearing the sign, "Computer." They cautiously opened the door, entered, and shut the door behind them. Lights came on automatically, and Nick moved forward. A large console with several computer screens and keyboards lay darkened. Nick flicked a switch, and the consoles came to life. "Let's see how good the rest of Ed's information is, shall we?"

Nick sat down at the console and typed a few characters on the keyboard.

"Hello," said the computer. "Would you be wanting to log on?"

"Yes," said Nick.

"Very well, sir. What is the password?"

Nick took a deep breath. "Submarine hamster."

"Access permitted."

Nick began to breath again, and put a diskette into a disk drive.

"Okay. Read that and execute."

The disk drive activity indicator came on.

To Annette, Nick said, "That should start Ed's, er, program."

"Completed," said the computer a moment later. "Any other requests?"

Nick and Annette looked at each other blankly for a moment. Nick shrugged and turned back to the computer. "Change password."

"Very well, sir. Please confirm the old password."

"Submarine hamster."

"Very well, sir. What is the new password?"

Nick thought for a moment. "McCormick sucks."

"Please repeat for confirmation."

"McCormick sucks."

"Completed. Any other request?"

"No. Log off."

"Very well, sir. Goodbye."

Nick retrieved the diskette and went back to the door with Annette. Nick opened it just a crack and peered out. They exited stealthily.

One floor up, they stopped and again pulled a stairwell door open a crack. This level opened onto a hallway much like the last. Lounging near a closed hallway door were three more guards. Nick let the door close lightly.

"What now?" Annette whispered.

Nick pulled a pellet out of a pocket. "This is the only thing we've haven't used so far, so it *must* be what we need."

"What is it?"

"A smoke bomb. I've got a couple of them, but one should be enough. Once it goes off and confuses them, I should be able to shoot them with tranquilizer darts."

"Well, we can't stop now."

They pulled the door open again, just a crack. When the guards were looking the other way, Nick quickly opened the door farther and threw the pellet along the floor.

The pellet came to rest right next to the trio of guards.

One of the guards cocked his head, looked around near his feet, and noticed the pellet. "What the hell is —"

The pellet exploded in a burst of smoke.

Nick opened the door all the way and shot each guard.

The smoke was dissipating already as Nick and Annette arrived. Nick pulled his real gun from behind his back, reconsidered, then kept his tranquilizer gun ready as he slowly opened the door to the room that had been under guard, a bedroom.

The room was dark. They crept into the room, stopping next to the bed where Mr. McCormick and presumably Mrs. McCormick lay asleep. Annette switched on a small lamp. Nick kept the tranquilizer gun ready, and he nudged Mr. McCormick's shoulder.

Mike McCormick jolted awake. "No, not OSHA! Not that!"

"Calm down, Mr. McCormick. It's just a dream."

"Thank God." McCormick blinked. "Who are you? And why are you in my bedroom, holding that gun? Damn it, I hate it when this happens!"

Downstairs in the monitoring room, a guard said, "Oh, God. We have a hell of a problem here."

The other guard joined him in looking at the monitor showing Nick holding a gun on Mr. McCormick. "Damn. Do we ignore it or tell him we've got a camera in there?"

Nick said, "We're not here to harm you, Mr. McCormick. We just want some answers, and we want to be left alone."

Mrs. McCormick stirred. Half asleep, she said, "Not *again*, Larry. Wait 'til Christmas."

McCormick said, "Go back to sleep, Cathy." To Nick and Annette he said, "What's this all about?"

There was a knock at the door.

"Get rid of them," Nick said. "Or you'll have more trouble on your hands." Nick held his tranquilizer gun on McCormick as McCormick went to the door and peeked through a privacy spy eye. He opened the door.

The guard at the door said, "I'm sorry to wake you, Mr. McCormick, but we have intruders. Several of the staff have been found unconscious."

"All right, Ellis. I'll stay right here." McCormick closed the door. "Now. Who the hell are you people?"

"My name is Nick Naught. This is Annette Taylor. Your goons kidnaped her brother. We've got him back, and we want you to lay off. Otherwise, a lawyer who's got the whole story will make it public."

"You're not Nick Knott."

"Why do you say that?"

"He's much older."

"So you're *not* after me? You're after someone else? Well *that* should simplify things a little."

As Nick finished speaking, the door burst open and four heavily armed guards piled into the room. Nick looked at his tranquilizer gun and sighed. He put the weapon on the table.

As the guards led Nick and Annette out at gunpoint, Mrs. McCormick stirred in bed. Sleepily she said, "Not again, Larry."

"Great work," said McCormick. "But how did you know they were in here?"

One of the guards said, "Can we talk about that a little later, sir?"

Chapter 22

IN the computer room once again, Annette and Nick stood, covered by guns held by M.O.B. guards. The door to the room opened. McCormick looked away from Nick as Paula Rosenberg and Dennis Cotton entered. Both looked sleepy. Rosenberg had her coat on inside out.

McCormick said, "What the hell's going on here, Rosenberg? This guy says he's Nick Knott."

"He can't be," Rosenberg said. "He's not old enough. You saw the picture, too."

"Sure, he is," Dennis said. "That's the guy on my form two-twelve." He took a folder from his pocket and withdrew his paper-work with Nick Naught's photo.

Rosenberg grabbed the photo and examined it. She turned to Dennis. "That's not the right Knott. This thing says Nick Naught. You idiot!"

"I'm an idiot? What are you talking about?" Dennis asked. "I can't help it if there was a screw-up. That's the guy I was told to get."

Jerry and Skid entered and joined the crowd. Jerry glared at Nick.

"What are *you two* doing here?" Rosenberg demanded.

Jerry said, "We found Ed Taylor sleeping in a car outside. We gave him another sedative and left him —" He did a double-take at Annette. "You got her already! Why didn't you tell us?"

"Got who?" Rosenberg asked.

"Annette Taylor. The guy's sister."

McCormick threw up his hands. "Wait a minute. Wait a minute! Things are getting way too confused. Let's start at the beginning." To Rosenberg, he said, "Where's *your* file photo on Nick Knott?"

"I don't have it with me. But the computer should have one."

"We'll see. At the rate things are going tonight, it'll be screwed up, too." McCormick turned to the computer terminal. "Log on."

"What is the password?" asked the computer.

"Submarine hamster," McCormick said confidently.

"What?"

"Submarine hamster," said McCormick more loudly.

"What?"

"Submarine hamster!" McCormick's cheeks turned pink.

"Warning! Warning! Unauthorized intruder alert. Password authorization failure." The computer paused. "One last chance. What is the password?"

Ultra calmly, between deep breaths, McCormick said, "Submarine hamster."

"Final warning! Final warning! Unauthorized intruder alert. Password authorization failure. Hostile takeover alert." A siren warble started up. "Destruction countdown commencing. One hundred. Ninety-nine —"

Pandemonium began.

"This can't be happening!" McCormick said.

The guards began to edge toward the door. "Stay right here," Rosenberg demanded.

The M.O.B. computer continued counting down.

McCormick pointed to a large panel. "The computer itself is through there! It's got its own power, and it's supposed to protect against a hostile takeover. We've got to switch it off before it blows up the bugging building!"

A guard rushed toward the panel and tried the handle. No luck. Another guard started to ram his shoulder against the panel. He was ineffective.

Jerry and Skid looked extremely nervous. They focused their

attention on McCormick. A third guard rushed toward the panel to help, leaving only one guard to watch Nick and Annette. The remaining guard was so engrossed in watching the commotion near the panel and looking nervously at his watch that Nick was able to take a short step while the guy was looking the other way.

Nick bashed the back of his fist into the guard's face. The guard slumped in Nick's arms, and Nick let him settle on the floor.

Nick grabbed the guard's gun. Together he and Annette slipped out the door they had come in through.

As Nick gently closed the door to the computer room behind them, he said, "You don't mind leaving the party early, do you?"

Annette said, "As long as you don't tell my parents."

They ran down the carpeted corridor and into the stairwell.

McCormick and his employees continued their attempts to break down the panel to get at the computer. The three guards ran in a group toward the panel, their shoulders together. They bounced off.

"Seventy-four. Seventy-three —"

Nick and Annette reached the first floor.

McCormick pleaded. "I'm a reasonable man. Now you be reasonable. I gave you the correct password."

"Sixty-eight. Sixty-seven —"

Nick and Annette ran along another corridor. They whipped around a corner and slammed into a guard who had been bringing Ed inside. The M.O.B. guard's head hit the wall, and he was out. Nick grabbed Ed, who was groggy again, and they continued their escape, a little more slowly.

McCormick's employees took another run at the panel. It seemed to give a little, but it held.

"Forty-two. Forty-two. Forty-two," said the computer. "Just kidding. Thirty-eight. Thirty-seven —"

Nick and Annette and Ed ran out the door and started across the street.

"Twenty-six. Twenty-five —"

Rosenberg said, "Boss, we'd better get out of here!"

"No! Keep at it!" To the computer, McCormick said, "Now listen to me very carefully. This is a mistake. I gave the correct password. Submarine hamster. Stop this right now!"

"Twenty-two. Twenty-one —"

"You stupid son of a bitch!" McCormick slammed his hand against the computer monitor.

Suddenly the computer countdown changed. The computer had been counting one number per second, like a shuttle launch. Now its voice was a blur as it counted down much more rapidly. "Fifteen twelve ten eight six four two one."

In the half second of agonizing silence following the completion of the countdown, Rosenberg gave McCormick a rude gesture and mouthed a very unflattering word.

The room they were in exploded.

Safely outside, Nick, Annette, and Ed watched as McCormick's house turned into a mass of light. Every room in the huge house was destroyed in a rippling series of explosions. The three survivors stumbled as the blasts shook the ground under their feet, but they were far enough away to survive. They got to their feet and looked back at the destruction. Nick and Annette put an arm around each other's waist.

A fire truck and an ambulance approached, sirens wailing, lights flashing. They sped past without stopping, already on their way to some other emergency.

Nick took a deep breath. "I think I could use a drink."

Chapter 23

THE drink in Nick's hand sloshed gently from side to side, and the ice tinkled against the glass. The dull roar of a plane in flight muffled conversations elsewhere in the passenger cabin. Next to Nick, Annette sat in the window seat.

A flight attendant handed Annette a drink and continued walking down the aisle, checking on passengers.

Out the window Nick could see the wing. A gaping hole showed where the main jet on that side used to be.

Annette took a sip of her drink, then sighed. "I think I'm really going to enjoy relaxing for a while."

"Me, too. Think of it as a gift from Jerry Pershing."

Annette looked puzzled, but before she could ask Nick to explain, the plane lurched and the pilot's voice came over the P.A. "Don't panic, ladies and gentlemen. We've developed a spot of engine trouble. I'm dreadfully sorry, but I'm afraid we're going to have to ditch."

In the sudden silence, Nick shook his head. "I hate it when this happens."

As the passengers panicked, the overhead compartments opened automatically, and oxygen masks dropped. The masks all looked like funny animal snouts, and the passengers didn't look at all dignified as they put their masks on.

Suddenly the vibration stopped, and the plane resumed normal flight.

The pilot's voice said, "Just kidding."

★ ★ ★

As the passengers deplaned, the stewardess was saying good-bye to everyone. Young native women gave leis to the arriving passengers.

Annette passed the cockpit and made the turn to exit the plane.

As Nick followed her past the cockpit, he pulled from his shirt pocket one of the unused smoke bomb pellets. He casually flipped it, Bogart style, into the cockpit and pulled the door closed. The door latched.

Nick exited the plane smiling, as the pellet exploded and smoke started to ooze through the seam next to the door. The view through the cockpit window was solid black.

Nick said, "Just kidding."

Nick and Annette walked down the ramp, arm in arm.

Chapter 24

ANNETTE reclined in a beach chair, wearing a lei.

Far away in the water, a police boat cut through the waves, running its siren. A cop's megaphoned voice was too far away to hear clearly. The gray beach extended in all directions from Annette's chair. If any remaining spots between occupied beach towels and chairs were larger than a square meter, they certainly weren't visible from where Annette sat. The beach looked endlessly crowded.

Next to Annette's chair, Nick bent over and balanced on one foot while he inspected his heel for evidence of dog.

As he did, Annette pinched him on the rear. She smiled with satisfaction at his startled expression.

Epilogue

Late at night in a deserted Los Angeles office, a telephone rang once. It rang again. And again. Finally the caller's attention span elapsed, and the phone stopped ringing.

The call would have been answered, but the phone answerer sat in the wastebasket, in even more tiny pieces than it had begun life with.

NAUGHT AGAIN

NICK Naught drove north on Central Boulevard, cruising smoothly through the night air like a glider sailing through the clouds. The evening was quiet; Nick hadn't heard a siren for more than five minutes. He passed a sign saying, "Can't read? *Literacy for All* can help."

Ahead the light turned yellow, then red. Beside him a dark red Flashfire slowed to a stop. The car was the same model as his, and Nick wondered if the driver had the same problems Nick did.

The silky sexy voice of his car computer spoke. "Wanna drag?"

"Get out of here." Nick shook his head.

In response, the engine revved. Nick's foot was an inch off the accelerator.

"Cut that out!"

"Oh, come on, Nick. What's the harm?"

God, Nick thought. Why couldn't I have just gotten one of the models with bad grammar? "Stop that, will you?" The car had been payment for a case, and with his current workload he couldn't afford to trade it in or get the AI replaced.

The engine revved again. Worse, the deep-throated throbbing from the car next to him suddenly revved into soprano.

"Dammit!" Nick said. "That guy's looking at me. Stop it."

Nick's engine revved again. "Oh, Nicky. Don't be such a spoil sport."

The Flashfire beside him revved in response, and Nick could see the other driver pounding on the dash. Why me, Lord? The other guy's car must have some of the same quirks.

"I absolutely refuse," Nick said. He would have put his foot down, but that was exactly what the car wanted.

Nick's engine revved again, and the engine in the red Flashfire revved in reply.

"I'm not kidding," Nick said. "I'll go out and buy a manual —"

The light changed. Tires screamed. The red Flashfire surged forward, and Nick's engine sucked all the gas it could through that tiny little fuel line. He was off. The pair of automobiles zoomed into the intersection.

"Watch it!" Nick cried as he almost clipped a yellow-jabbing Jeep that sped through after the light had turned. "Dammit, stop!" Nick jammed his foot on the brake, but the car computer had obviously played some trick with the antiskid system to tell the brakes they weren't needed right at the moment.

"Come on," Nick said as they flashed past a string of parked cars and the other Flashfire started to pull ahead. "My PI license is already in trouble. I can't afford to lose my driver's license. Do you know how long I had to wait in line for that sucker?"

The car was silent, no doubt devoting all its energy to the race. The other Flashfire shifted, lost a few meters in the process, and Nick's car topped sixty. Nick began concentrating on the steering wheel.

The other Flashfire hit its stride and began to pull ahead slowly now, the driver still pounding on the dash.

A slow-moving street-cleaner ahead finally decided it was dark enough to turn on its lights. Twin red running lights flared in the Flashfire's path. The car didn't slow down.

The driver hunched up his shoulder, and a moment later sparks flew near the steering wheel. The guy had fired a shot into the dash.

As the red Flashfire swerved around the street cleaner, another car began to back onto the road ahead. The Flashfire swerved again.

The Flashfire driver nearly made it, but at the last instant clipped the car backing onto the boulevard. The red automobile started a spin straight down the center of the road. The Flashfire skidded through almost 360 degrees. While the car was moving sideways, still turning so that in another three seconds it would be pointed straight down the road again, it hit a big pothole.

In apparent slow motion, the red Flashfire flipped. It was probably still moving at near a hundred, and it tumbled at least a half-dozen times as it gradually slowed down. Nick's car finally relinquished control and reacted to Nick's foot holding the brake pedal to the floor. "I hope you're happy now," Nick said as the car began to slow down.

Nick pulled to a stop fifty feet from the red Flashfire, which had come to rest on its crinkled roof. He was nervous about the possibility of an explosion, but he ran to the car and managed to force open a door. Inside the wreck, the car voice was saying over and over, "I told you, you should have put your seat belt on."

The driver's body had been thrown into the back seat, but apparently not before it had been smashed against the steering column. Blood oozed from a huge bloody hole in the driver's chest. Nick felt sick. From force of habit rather than hope, he reached for the guy's wrist, trying to avoid getting blood on himself. No pulse. Nick finally realized nothing was going to revive this guy.

The man's silencer-equipped gun lay on the bloody roof of the car. Nick pulled the body from the car and carried it far enough away that he should be safe if the car exploded. By this time porch lights had come on in front of several of the nearby houses.

The driver wore a mummy shirt, a long strip of narrow cloth wound around his torso until the top end was tucked in at his neck. Over the shirt he wore a light jacket that no longer adequately concealed the shoulder holster. Nick set the body on the sidewalk and propped it up long enough to dig out the man's wallet. A loud explosion suddenly sounded from the upturned wreck, but it was only the air-bag finally letting go.

Nick went back to his search, having no real reason except his latent PI tendencies and unmanageable curiosity, this time activated by the silencer on the guy's gun. The man's ID said he was Evan Jiffon, birth date 20 July 1982, and gave an address on Harper Lane. He had more teeth in his picture than he did now. Nick automatically checked the "secret compartment," still curious about why, if all men bought wallets with "secret compartments," how anyone would think it was safe. From the compartment, Nick pulled a dark piece of paper.

He unfolded the paper and read the words, but they made no sense to him. A suicide note? He read farther. Something was definitely wrong. This guy hadn't died of the drug overdose referenced in the note. And Nick had real trouble picturing this guy with a name like Sylvia.

Nick kept the note, returned the wallet, and let the body flop onto its back. He closed the jacket over the worst of the chest wound, and noticed something stuck between mummy-shirt layers. Nick pulled out a parking receipt from a local garage.

"Is he all right?" asked someone over Nick's shoulder. The first neighbor had arrived, a bearded guy wearing a t-shirt over his beer gut. Not too far behind him, the driver of the car that had been clipped was finally on his way.

"Shouldn't you be calling nine-one-one?" Nick asked. He put the parking receipt back where he had found it.

"Already got a claim number. The recording said it would be about two hours."

"Great," Nick said as he palmed the note. "At least this guy isn't going to be impatient."

"You mean he's —"

"He's firing fewer neurons than a member of congress. He's

dead."

"God. He looks so lifelike."

Nick looked up at the man. He stood up and got blood flowing through his legs again. Nick looked down at the driver, then back at the neighbor and said, "As a matter of fact, so do you."

As the man scratched his head, Nick took a card from his wallet and handed it to the man. "If the nine-one-one recording says two hours, it'll be more like four. Have the police call me. All I can tell them is that the guy was speeding and took a bad turn."

Back in Nick's car, he slid the key into the ignition, and the car voice said, "Ohhh, Nicky. Do that again."

★   ★   ★

Nick pulled to a stop on Harper Lane, about four houses down from the address on Evan Jiffon's driver's license. The narrow road wound up into trees so thick that from where he sat he could see five mailboxes, but only one house. Down the street, a car anti-theft alarm began to *whoop whoop-whoop* with no indication that anyone was even near the car. Nick wondered if he should get stickers for *his* car that said, "No alarm on board," and start leaving the key in the ignition. In fact, maybe he should leave some money on the dash.

The alarm from the parked car kept going, and the loud noise apparently triggered the alarm in the car next to it. The pair of cars wailed back and forth like animals in heat. Nick pulled back onto the street and drove until he was about five houses past his destination. He parked. He was about to open his door when he suddenly stopped and said, "Don't listen to the radio while I'm gone, all right? I don't want to attract attention."

The car voice was silent for a moment. "If I don't, can we listen to what *I* want to next time?"

Nick pushed the heel of his hand against his forehead. "Yes."

"What was that?"

Nick clenched his teeth. "*Yes.*" He got so *damn* tired of those old Jan and Dean and Beach Boys hot rod songs.

The night was quiet except for a few very distant sirens. A gentle breeze came from the north, carrying the smell of rain and just a hint of cordite. Nick walked casually down the road, turned in at Jiffon's mailbox, and walked halfway up the sidewalk before scooting off into the darkness, heading toward the side of the house.

Houses in this neighborhood might have silent alarms hooked to the police department, but if the nine-one-one recording said two hours to respond to a traffic death, Nick could probably move in and never see a cop for the first three months.

Between Jiffon's house and his neighbor's were enough trees and bushes to make Nick feel fairly comfortable. He reached a ground-floor window and found it locked. He backed away from the house, looking up, and backed into a tree limb. On the second floor, just above the narrow ledge of a roof, a window was open a couple of inches.

Nick pulled himself up to the top of the wooden fence surrounding the back yard, and from there scrambled to the narrow section of roof. He crept forward, leaning against the side of the house, listening for noise coming from inside. He heard nothing.

He pulled the window slowly open. Fortunately it had no screen. Still hearing nothing from inside, Nick stepped through the opening and onto a hardwood floor. Even in the dim light, Nick could see the room was empty. He stayed where he was, letting his ears adjust to the inside noises. He still heard nothing that made him think the house was occupied.

He crept around the perimeter of the room, wanting to avoid any creaking floorboards, and at the door, he listened again. Nothing.

On this floor was a bathroom right across the hall, and two

more bedrooms. Stairs led down to the main floor. Nick moved to the closest bedroom and found a sparsely furnished room containing only a bed and a chair. The other bedroom was as empty as the one he had come in through.

The stairs presented a problem. If he crept down the stairs, there was nothing to prevent someone from getting a nice long look at his feet and blowing him away when he came even lower. Nick lay on his stomach and lowered his head to the top step. From there he could see a little of the kitchen floor and an empty hallway. He was especially happy that he didn't see any dog dishes. Being a private eye meant having an appreciation for the small things in life.

He inched down a step, like an awkward snake. He saw more kitchen floor, still unoccupied. He moved another step, suddenly afraid he would accidentally slide the rest of the way down, hitting his head on each step and then slamming his head against the wall. He tried to back up the stairs.

No leverage. He had already come down too far. He twisted and grabbed one of the banister supports. It creaked.

Nick froze. His ears cranked up to maximum sensitivity, and the hairs on the back of his neck extended until they seemed to be perfectly straight.

He really had to get a grip on his curiosity. Instead of sneaking around here, he could have been happily cruising Muholland, listening to the melodic strains of "Drag City."

Still no sounds came from the downstairs. Nick pulled himself around into sitting position and crept down the stairs that way.

The kitchen really was deserted. Nick moved carefully down the hall and found a dark and deserted living room and an unoccupied bathroom. Adjacent to the bathroom was an empty bedroom and an empty den. The house was unoccupied, unless someone was hiding in a closet, and Nick wasn't going to spend his time looking.

The den was sparsely furnished, too. A desk, a chair, and a waste-basket were the only blemishes on the hardwood floor. On top of the desk were a few bills and a letter opener. Inside the top desk drawer was the front section of a recent newspaper.

Nick opened the newspaper and set it on the desktop. The head-line said, "Bridge Collapses — Design Error Blamed." In the lower right corner was the story of Ted Harley's death. Harley had been a rich developer whose last physical said he was in good health, but the heart attack made the diagnosis seem questionable. Nick scanned the other stories and was about to put the newspaper back when he spotted a name in the Harley story. Ted Harley's daughter's name was Sylvia. According to the story, at least when it had come out a week ago, Sylvia was alive.

"*Pssst!*" The sound came from behind him.

Nick jumped a foot. As soon as he hit the ground, he looked around wildly. He saw no one.

"Pssst!" The sound came again.

Nick finally realized it was the telephone. *Damn.*

"Pssst!"

Nick's curiosity went into overdrive, and he picked up the receiver. "Yeah."

"You done already?" asked a smooth voice.

Nick hesitated. "Yeah."

"Why didn't you call?"

"I was going to."

This time the caller hesitated. "If this is really you, call *me* back." *Click.*

Damn. For all Nick knew, the voice on the phone could belong to the nextdoor neighbor. He had to get out of there.

Nick left by the front door. He grimaced as he realized it had been unlocked.

*   *   *

A phone booth in a mini-mall a mile away held a phone book with half its pages missing, but the book still contained the one page Nick needed.

Nick drove south on Lincoln, the cool night air blowing in through the open window. He clenched his teeth as for the third time in a row the radio began to play "Little Deuce Coupe."

Nick pulled up to the curb a couple of houses down from the address the phone book had shown for Sylvia Harley. He got out of the car and approached the house, a house much more expensive than Jiffon's place. This one sported a high, peaked ceiling, with an expanse of windows in the triangle formed by the eaves. The front door was a double door, the kind that made him unsure which side to knock on.

Nick found the bell and heard it chime faintly somewhere inside.

He heard the *click click click* of heels inside before the door opened and revealed an attractive blonde about two inches taller than Nick. Her eyes were dark, her lipstick bright, and she was dressed in a business suit. Just to the left of her mouth was a small mole, not quite covered with makeup.

"I'm glad you're here," she said. "I was afraid I'd gotten the night wrong. Can we take your car? Normally I'd offer, but mine's in the shop again."

Nick hesitated. "Sure." He knew so little about what was going on, the woman was about his only hope. Perhaps she'd let a few clues drop before she realized Nick wasn't the person she'd been expecting.

He backed up as the woman came through the door and locked it behind her. The moving door pushed some of her perfume toward him. He couldn't remember the name, but it was the same fragrance his date for the senior prom had worn. He was sure of it.

"I'm down this way, er, my car is. I must have read the street numbers wrong."

As they reached the car, it was playing "Sting Ray."

Nick held the door open for the woman he assumed was Sylvia Harley.

As he got around to his door, opened it, and got in, the feminine car voice said, "Bimbo alert at three o'clock."

The woman opened her lips and started to say something when Nick interrupted. "Just ignore the car, okay? It was in the shop a couple of months ago, and the AI system has been even flakier than normal ever since."

"I understand. So, which one do you want to see first?"

Nick hesitated. "You decide."

"Let's go up to Evans then."

Nick nodded. To the car he said, "Can you play something else?"

The car started "Drag City."

Nick looked at the woman. "It's a long story."

"It's all right. I like it."

Nick bit his tongue as the radio volume shot up.

★　　★　　★

The car cut through the night as Nick wondered what to say next. Now that she couldn't easily retreat to her house if he'd made an identity mistake, he said, "Which way now, Sylvia?"

"Left, then take a right two blocks up."

Good. She must in fact be Sylvia Harley.

Nick pulled up in front of a house that was probably eighty years old. It was dark but for the single yellow porch lamp.

At the door, Sylvia unlocked a lock-box and withdrew a key that opened the front door. Inside she flipped on the foyer light, and Nick followed her in.

"Living room," she said. "The floors have just been resurfaced. I love hardwood floors."

By now Nick had a pretty good idea that this house wasn't going to offer any clues, and it would be only minutes before Sylvia figured out he wasn't who he was pretending to be, whoever that was.

"All new appliances in the kitchen two years ago," she said.

"Sylvia, can we stop for just a second?"

"Yes?"

"Look, I've got to ask you a question. This is maybe going to scare you a little, but I'm no threat to you. Honestly."

Sylvia squinted at him and retreated a couple of steps. "You're not really interested in buying, are you?"

"I'm not the guy who scheduled this appointment. And I think there's something you should know."

Sylvia started edging toward to the front door. "Who the hell are you?"

"I'm Nick Naught. I'm a private eye."

Sylvia looked at him for a long moment. "You don't mind if we talk on the sidewalk out front, do you?"

"That would be fine," Nick said, understanding her fears completely.

A street lamp half a block away assisted the moonlight, and Sylvia seemed to relax.

"I'm going to take a note from my pocket," Nick said. "I didn't write this, but I'd like to know a little more about the note. What it says may upset you, but I didn't write it."

"I got it. You didn't write it."

"Exactly."

Nick retrieved the suicide note, unfolded it, and handed it to her.

"I can't read it in this light. What does it say?" She gave the note back to him.

"It, ah, says, 'I can't take it anymore.' It goes on to say the writer would rather be dead than to go on living with the humiliation. And not to bother with revival attempts, because the dose is ten times higher than a fatal dose. It's signed, 'Sylvia.'"

Sylvia sucked in her breath. She grabbed the note, moved to the car, and opened the door. "Stay away from me. I'll scream."

Nick backed up a couple of paces. "I didn't write that —"

Sylvia read the note in the glow of the dome light. "Well, I sure as hell didn't, either. But it looks like my handwriting. What's going on?"

"I'll tell you all I know. I found that note on a dead man earlier tonight. I searched his house and I found a newspaper article about your dad's death. It mentioned your name, so I put two and two together."

"This isn't making any sense." Sylvia's voice was pinched, nervous.

"I know. I thought maybe you could help me understand what's going on. It seems maybe you're in trouble."

"I don't intend to kill myself."

"I know that. Relax a minute and think things through. Someone *else* may want you dead. That note would be what the killer left behind."

"No one would want me dead. That's idiotic."

"Who did you have an appointment with tonight?"

"A guy named Max Jericho."

"Ever see him?"

"No. He called me up a couple of days ago."

"That could be the guy who wrote that note."

"A guy who's dead now? How did that happen?"

Nick spread his hands. "It's kind of a long boring story."

"But you came across his body and you found this note on him?"

"Right. He didn't look like a Sylvia, so I got curious."

"And if that guy hadn't died tonight, I might be dead right now?"

"It's a possibility."

Sylvia sagged against the car. "God."

"So, no one you know of has a reason to want you dead?"

"No! For that matter, did you kill this guy?"

"No. He, uh, died in a traffic accident."

"God, first my father dies, and now someone wants me dead?"

"I know. Really a rotten month. Do you know an Evan Jiffon?"

"No. That's the name of the guy who died?"

"Yeah."

"Never heard of him."

"Anything unusual about this last month or two?"

"You mean other than having my father die and finding out he paid for one of those meat lockers?"

"Meat locker? You mean a cryo-crypt?"

"Yeah. Evergreen Deep Freeze."

"Evergreen? I thought if you froze hamburger, having it turn green was a bad sign."

"I don't think that's exactly the image they had in mind." She hesitated. "I went up to see him. He had even paid for a contract for me."

"So when you die, you wind up in the freezer, too?"

"You'd make a charming undertaker."

"Sorry. I'm preoccupied. None of this is making much sense to me."

Sylvia shivered. "Take me home, will you?"

"You trust me?"

"409" blared from the car as Sylvia looked at it and said, "No killer would have a car like this."

Nick wasn't too sure about that.

★　　★　　★

Nick slowed to a stop in front of Sylvia's home. "I really do think you'd be better off with some kind of protection."

Sylvia shook her head again. "I know you mean well, but I can't just bring a detective along on whenever I show a house. I'll be more careful about making sure someone else always knows when I'm going out, and I'll make sure anyone I show a house to knows that a friend is keeping track."

"At least let someone guard your house. If not me, pick someone from the book, or I can recommend a couple of people."

"The house is secure. I've got very good locks, and an expensive alarm system." Sylvia hesitated. "You wouldn't go through such an elaborate con job just to get business, would you?"

"It's no con job," Nick said. He looked straight at her.

Sylvia opened the car door. "All right. I believe you. Look, I'll be careful, and if anything funny happens, I'll call you."

"Okay." Nick didn't like it, but he couldn't really force protection on her.

"Good night," she said.

"Good night," said Nick.

"Close the door, will you?" said the car.

Nick watched Sylvia enter her house safely, then drove away slowly. The car said, "I could have won that race if I had good tires. How about some new HR-15s, Nicky?"

★　　★　　★

Two days later, Nick scanned the morning paper.

"Uh oh." He leaned closer to the paper and felt sick. "Damn it!"

Sylvia Harley was dead. The paper said her body had been discovered by the maid. Apparently Sylvia had slipped in the bath and hit her head hard enough to knock her unconscious, and she had drowned. Sure, and General Motors management donated to the union strike fund.

So despite Sylvia taking more precautions, they had gotten to her. The frustration built up in Nick until he couldn't ignore it. He had to do something.

He'd visit Evergreen. He might not learn anything, but he had to make the attempt.

Nick rinsed his coffee cup, and water swirled down the drain as he briefly considered taking a cab.

★   ★   ★

As Nick drove past Fundamentally High School, a lone protester paced before the main doors. The old woman's placard read, "Put science back in education." Last week a letter on the editorial page had suggested that things wouldn't be so bad if the schools weren't turning out so many uneducated idiots. Today, probably in sympathy with the letter, someone had posted a large sign saying, "School Zone — 75 MPH."

Nick pulled up in front of Evergreen Deep Freeze. The building looked more like a big old mansion than a public meat locker. The tasteful and subdued letters EDF were all Nick saw at first that told him he was in the right place. And not a block away was the parking garage the dead man had a receipt from.

At the end of a long trek up a carefully edged sidewalk slicing through a putting-green lawn, Nick saw the script lettering next to the door saying EDF did indeed stand for what he thought it stood for.

He opened the door and walked in. The carpet felt as thick as the grass had looked. The music was soft and apparently meant to be soothing, a musak version of "In my Room" by the Beach Boys.

A tall man with hollow cheeks appeared through a curtain formed of tapestry strips. "May I help you, sir?" In another century, he could well have been a butler. His nose hairs made his mustache fuller. His voice reminded Nick of the voice on Jiffon's phone.

"Yes. I came to see Sylvia Harley."

"I'm sorry, sir. Only immediate family members are allowed."

"Well, I'm almost immediate family. We were engaged."

"I'm sorry, sir —"

"And I was thinking of paying for storage for myself in the event that something should happen to me."

"Well, sir, seeing as how you were so close to Ms. Sylvia. I'm Alvin Hodges."

Alvin led Nick through a doorway at the back of the house and along a corridor angling toward the rear of the lot, where a more modern building lay. Framed pictures lined the corridor wall, presumably all of them "befores." Nick recognized at least four people he'd seen on the society pages. At one of the picture, he paused. "So Bentley Parsons is a client, too?"

"Yes, sir. His body was fairly badly crushed by a hit-and-run driver, but his brain is in tip-top shape. As soon as medical science is ready for brain transplants, Mr. Parsons will be ready to come in out of the cold." Alvin chuckled at what he must have thought was a joke.

"But Sylvia won't have to wait that long, will she?"

"I'm afraid she will, sir. You no doubt know that she drowned. As it turns out, she was found before her brain suffered irreversible damage. Unfortunately, when the rescue team attempted open heart massage, they did enough damage to her heart and lungs that, even if she were alive, she'd need transplants. Besides that, all we at Evergreen preserve is the head along with the brain stem and the upper section of the spinal cord. None of these people will be revived until medical science can replace most of the rest of the body, and until we know much more about the aging process. I hope that with the progress they're making today, they'll be revived and up and around in perhaps twenty years."

"That's seems like a long time."

Alvin nodded.

They walked in silence a few paces and Nick said, "So, how long have you folks been in business? I sure wish you'd been around when my brother —"

"About a year, sir. When your brother —"

"I'd rather not talk about it."

"Certainly, sir. Ah, here we are."

Alvin led Nick through another door, this one considerably more sturdy than the first door. The room beyond was a little like a laundromat, but much colder and with no coin slots. Rows of cabinets lined the floor, and Nick could see his breath in the air.

Nick stopped in front of the first cabinet and peered through the slanting oval window at the top. "I can't see anything."

"That's where we keep the Popsicles, sir."

"That's what you call them?"

"No." The man snapped the latch and opened the front of the cabinet. He withdrew a fudgesicle and offered it to Nick.

"Oh, I see. All right. Thanks."

Nick tore open the wrapper and started nibbling on the fudgesicle as they walked down the aisle. Dead faces stared through the frosty windows.

"Miss Sylvia is right here," said Alvin. He rested his fingers on top of a cabinet, and Nick moved closer. As Nick neared the glass, Alvin started to remove his hand from the frosty sheen on the cold cabinet top. He couldn't; his fingers were stuck.

Nick saw the man's dilemma and winced. "Here, let me help."

He gave Alvin's hand a sharp pull, and the fingers came loose from the cabinet with a pitiful ripping noise. Two patches of skin stayed on the ice.

"Ah, sorry about that," Nick said.

Nick moved back to Sylvia's cabinet and noticed her name on a tag just under the oval window. The window was slightly frosty. Nick wiped away some frost and condensation and peered through the window. He sucked in a deep breath as he saw Sylvia's face, small mole and all, her eyes closed, her skin tinged lightly blue.

Nick stood up. "Why does she look so far away from the window? The cabinet doesn't even look that deep."

"For safety, the head is placed well away from the observation port. Ms. Harley's head is actually about halfway between the floor and the window, facing the rear of the cabinet. A mirror at the rear lets us see her face. We have numerous sensors installed in each cabinet, but the observation port lets the family see their loved one, and lets us make occasional visual checks."

"Could I see her father, too? We were friends."

"Surely, sir."

As Alvin escorted Nick along the aisle, Nick glanced at more of the faces and memorized several of the other names. "What happens in the case of someone with a severe head wound?"

"Typically such victims are not candidates for Evergreen. But the lucky ones, the ones whose brains are intact, will no doubt be forever grateful to Evergreen. When they finally awake, they may well be immortal."

Nick didn't comment on the choice of the word "lucky." Seconds later they arrived at Ted Harley's cabinet. Nick saw the face from the newspaper photo, hair combed just the same way, with Harley looking as though he were just taking a quick nap. Nick wondered if sutures inside Harley's lips held them closed as if the body were at a funeral.

"God, I just can't believe they're both gone," Nick said finally.

"I know exactly how you feel, sir."

Right, thought Nick. The musak had switched to Simon and Garfunkle's "Sounds of Silence."

Alvin went on. "But when they awake, they will have the last laugh. They will never have felt better."

"Well, thanks for letting me see them."

"You're quite welcome. As long as you're here, you said you'd like to take a brochure that explains our services?"

"Yes, of course."

Back in the lobby, Alvin handed Nick a letter-sized file folder full of sales literature. "Here you are, Mr. —"

"Rice. Edgar Rice."

★   ★   ★

"Nick Naught Private Investigations," Nick said into the phone.

"Jeez, Nick. Why don't you get an answering machine? I tried to get you all afternoon," said Ricardo, a buddy of Nick's who did computer searches for him. Nick often did enough legwork that he didn't need Ricardo as much, but for the last few days he hadn't felt much like driving.

"It's a long story. What do you have?"

"I got answers back on all those names." Ricardo was a terrific researcher. Nick wouldn't have minded having Ricardo helping him with some of the actual fieldwork, too, but Ricardo's idea of living dangerously was buying a car with a side mirror that didn't say, "Objects in the mirror are closer than they appear."

"And? Anything in common?"

"A little. They're all A-plus ratings or better."

"Makes sense. Evergreen's probably not cheap. What else?"

"They all checked out during the last year."

"Okay. Evergreen's probably fairly new, so that's not suspicious."

"Their credit ratings are zilched out."

"They're all dead. What did you expect?"

"I know that. But credit reports usually take a while to wind down. The accounts go into an estate fund, and creditors wait in line to get fed. These folks all had major accounts at Rock Solid S&L, and as soon as they died the account balances went into century trust funds set up for when they thaw. They're leaving enough behind to pay bills, but these people found a way to take it with them. There's no law saying a dead guy can't make money in the bank."

"Now that's interesting," said Nick. "I bet if they stay frozen long enough, they'll all be billionaires when they get out."

"If you were sure you'd come back healthy and young and rich, I can see where some people might volunteer — not even wait for an accident. I remember the days when I was a kid, and the cops would come in an hour or two if you called them. It would be nice to think that someday in the future things won't be quite so messed up. Maybe these folks thought the same thing."

Nick hesitated. "What kind of health were they in?"

The line was silent for a moment. "They're dead, Nick. Think about it."

"I know that. I mean in general were they old people near death, or people with terminal illnesses, or what?"

"Oh. Just a sec." Moments later Ricardo was back on the line. "That's funny. If their medical-insurance premiums are any guide, aside from a few people who knew they were dying, the rest were all in perfect health."

★   ★   ★

Nick did some more checking from his office that evening.

Evergreen was ten months old and financially very stable. Nick tried to get info on the trust funds set up for the Evergreen residents in deep freeze, but couldn't.

He sat at his desk feeling confused. Often when he was working on a case, at some point he'd finally latch onto the key fact that made everything else start to make sense, and so far with this case he hadn't. He picked up the newspaper with the story about Sylvia and stared at her picture. She looked just like she had at Evergreen except that in the newspaper photo her eyes were open.

Nick put the paper back on the desk and thought some more. And then suddenly he was up and moving, out of the office and toward the elevator.

His car greeted him as he slid behind the wheel. "Where have you been, Nicky? It's lonely out here."

"I've been busy, okay?"

"Okay," said the car. It was silent a moment. "You know, new tires would increase your gas mileage and make me a lot safer on wet streets."

★   ★   ★

Nick had to park several blocks away from Evergreen, just in case the sound from the radio carried. On the walk from the car, even though he stayed on the sidewalks, he set off a half-dozen overly sensitive car alarms that cried "Stand back from the car!" and "Stop, thief!" in his trail. A block later he passed an unoccupied Cadillac playing Wagner.

At the back of the group of Evergreen buildings was an idling hearse with no driver. Nick cautiously moved closer to the rear door of the building. It was propped open with a rock. Nick peered through the gap and saw movement. Instead of going inside, he peeled a strip of tape from a small roll in his pocket and hastily taped the latch bolt so it couldn't extend into the striker plate when the door closed. He moved back along the side of the building until he reached some shrubbery that would provide adequate concealment.

Minutes later the hearse driver came back out. She kicked the rock way and let the door fall closed. Twin red taillights disappeared into the darkening night, and Nick decided he'd better play safe and wait for a while. He was pretty sure he still knew how to recognize poison ivy, and he was reasonably sure this wasn't it.

★   ★   ★

Nick woke with a start, almost like he was back in one of the boring classes he'd had in any number of schools. An ant had just bitten him on the nose. He squashed the ant between finger and thumb and didn't feel guilty in the slightest. His back was sore, and his wallet and tool kit pressed into his rear like twin tumors.

The night was dark and still, and the air smelled of the plants nearby. Nick stretched and yawned.

A single floodlight illuminated the small parking lot, which was fortunately empty. Nick reached the back door, and it opened easily.

A vacant corridor awaited. It had been thoughtfully carpeted to keep the noise down. Nick moved quietly inside and let the door close gently behind him. He could smell one of his least pleasant odors of high school: formaldehyde.

The first door Nick came to was locked, but he got it open with a credit card. Too bad the room turned out to be just a bathroom. These people must lock everything.

The next door was locked, too. Fortunately this lock, also, was a blue-light special. Beyond the door lay a doctor's office, or at least it looked vaguely like one, but for the power tools near the coffin-sized operating table with gutters along the sides. A large refrigerator stood near one corner. Inside were a number of beakers, each with a different specimen floating inside. Nick was pretty sure one was a heart, but he couldn't tell a spleen from a kidney or a thyroid gland. As he closed the door, he suddenly remembered the recent *Global Inquirer* article about the woman who'd received an appendix transplant.

So, if his gut reaction were correct, Evergreen made some pocket change by selling organs retrieved before they finished with the bodies. Nick wondered if that money went into the victims' trust funds, but he suspected the answer was no. Or, as Alvin would probably say, assuredly not.

At the next door, Nick decided Evergreen must have gotten a quantity discount on locks. This room felt warmer than the others. On the far wall was the explanation. Heavy iron doors with well-insulated handles opened onto a crematorium furnace. That explained where the unused parts of the bodies went. Nick wondered if they had to abide by pollution-alert no-burn days. Lately there had been at least twenty-seven of them a month, so on the occasional approved burning day, the sun usually disappeared by noon.

The corridor was as quiet as ever when Nick eased back into it. The door across the hall yielded to his efforts, and beyond it lay the rear of the large room Nick had visited with Alvin. Evergreen must shut off the visitors' heat at night, because the room felt even colder than it had earlier. His breath fogged the air. He kept his head low as he moved down a couple of rows so he could sit on the floor and be out of sight of both doors.

He sat next to one of the refrigerated units and grabbed the tool kit from his pocket. The nameplate on the unit identified the occupant as Morton Westheimmer. With the tiny flashlight, Nick got back to his feet and crouched next to the observation window. He wiped away frost and condensation and peered inside. The face of a slumbering forty-year-old man inside reminded Nick of one of his laziest teachers back in school.

Nick twisted on the flashlight and directed the beam inside. He moved it from side to side but the beam didn't brighten the sleeping face. Nick had a sudden thought about one-way glass and dismissed it.

Near the bottom of the cabinet was a panel that ran the width of the unit, held in place with eight torque screws. Nick used his tool and a couple of minutes later the panel suddenly sagged on one side as Nick got ready to take out the last screw. Inside the enclosure was a compressor, no doubt part of the cooling system, and next to it was an electrical plug inserted in a socket in the floor.

Nick drew in a breath, planning to remove the plug for only a couple of seconds. Surely the insulation in the unit would prevent any real damage. He pulled the plug. The compressor went right on running.

Nick looked more closely at the inside of the box. Sure enough, they had installed an uninterruptible power supply. Evergreen certainly wouldn't want to be off the air during a power failure.

He reached into the cabinet, found the recessed switch, and flicked it off. The compressor died. Rapidly Nick raised his head and peered through the observation window. He saw nothing. He flicked on his tiny light. The inside of the cabinet was empty.

"I'll be damned," Nick said softly.

"You never can tell," said a voice behind him.

Nick turned carefully, slowly, keeping his hands visible.

Alvin stood just on the other side of a row of cabinets. With him were two men who looked more like businessmen than guards, but all three men held pistols pointed at Nick.

Nick didn't stand to gain anything by playing dumb. "Holograms, huh? So this whole thing is just a big con game to get estate money from rich victims?"

Alvin said, "Actually, I thought we'd last longer than we did.

But we have made an obscene amount of money already, so I guess all's well that ends well. I am curious about what tipped you off, though. I promise we'll be harder on you if you don't tell us."

Nick considered that for a moment. "They all looked just like their pictures."

"That's bad?"

"I mean exactly like their pictures. Sylvia's mole was on the same side. Ted Harley had his hair parted on the correct side."

"So?"

"So, you told me the heads face the rear and a mirror lets people outside see them. You look in a mirror and tell me if your hair is still parted on the same side."

Alvin gritted his teeth. "Thank you, Mr. Rice. Although I don't suppose your real name is Rice."

"Naught."

"I said that."

"Nick Naught. That's my name."

"I bet that was fun growing up with."

"Oh, yeah."

One of the men with Alvin started getting visibly impatient, shifting from one foot to the other. He looked like one of the heavyweights on "Boxing for Dollars."

"Well, Mr. Naught, I guess we'd better get started," said Alvin.

"Started?"

"You don't have a car in the lot."

"No."

"But no doubt you have one close by. And we don't want it found near here. Mr. McCarthy will go with you to your car and bring you back here." Alvin indicated the impatient man with no neck.

"And why should I do that?"

"Hope springs eternal. Have you forgotten? If you don't do it, we'll kill you right now and look up your license plate number on our own. If you help us, you stay alive longer, and I'm sure that will motivate you."

"Okay, let's go." Nick stood up slowly. "Just don't use anymore homilies on me. I don't think I can take it."

Alvin frowned. "Just a moment." While Alvin's silent helpers held their guns on Nick, Alvin found and removed Nick's pistol. "There now. I think you're ready."

Nick trudged toward the back of the complex, trying to figure out how to get away from the silent man following him with a gun. They went out, through the parking lot, and onto the dark street, quiet but for the sound of a few distant sirens and car radios.

They walked five blocks before the man behind him said anything. "I think you're trying to be funny. I'm not going to follow you around the neighborhood until dawn. We get to your car in ten minutes, or we don't get to it at all."

Nick stopped, then turned back the way they had come. A block later they reached Nick's car. The windows were all the way up, but Nick could easily hear "Little GTO" playing inside.

"Here we are," Nick said.

"You drive." The man held his gun on Nick as he got into the passenger seat and Nick slipped behind the wheel.

"Turn that crap off," Nick said as he started the engine.

The radio volume dropped. "Why?" asked the car.

"You'd better get used to playing something else," Nick said as he pulled into the deserted street.

"Why?"

"Because you're going to have a new owner soon, and probably no one else will put up with this." Almost anyone else would probably have the money to completely replace the car computer.

"Why?"

"Is that all it can say?" asked Nick's heavyweight passenger.

"Because this guy is planning to kill me," said Nick.

"Why?" asked the car.

"Does it really matter —" Nick was saying when suddenly an explosion sounded and the passenger-side air-bag burst in the face of the man with the gun. Nick jammed on the brakes and hit the heel of his hand as hard as he could against his captor's temple. The man's head jerked over and smacked hard against the side window. Seconds later Nick had the man's gun in his hand.

"Excellent work!" Nick shouted.

"Thank you," said the car. "But you're going to owe me."

★   ★   ★

Nick knelt and placed the dozen roses on Sylvia's grave.

"I'm sorry, Sylvia. No one should have to die for such a senseless reason. Maybe now you can at least sleep a little easier."

Nick walked slowly back toward his car in the cool morning air. When he was almost there, an old woman said loudly, "I think that's disgraceful."

She must have been talking about the strains of "Dead Man's Curve" seeping through Nick's car doors and windows.

Nick spread his hands helplessly.

The woman scowled at him as he drove away.

Nick still felt depressed about Sylvia's death as he drove, but he did feel a sense of accomplishment in getting Evergreen shut down. The police had actually arrived fairly promptly, and Ricardo had been able to verify that all the trust funds set up for the victims at Rock Solid S&L had been funneled into Evergreen. Alvin and his friends would be in a different kind of deep freeze for a long time.

"So, Nick," said the car. "What about that new fuel injection system?"

"Give me a break. Weren't the new tires enough? How long am I going to have to pay?"

The car was silent for a moment. "I know your MasterCard number."

"God." Nick massaged his temples.

Seconds later, a deep rumbling sounded from behind the car. In the rear-view mirror appeared a huge band of mean-looking bikers. The two guys in front had so many tattoos their skin looked like blueprints. Chains hung from their necks, and pieces of food were stuck between their teeth. Or maybe those were bugs stuck in their teeth. A few more bikers sped past before the car said innocently, "Come on, Nicky. You wouldn't want the horn to stick, would you?"

CPSIA information can be obtained at www.ICGtesting.com
Printed in the USA
BVOW031505070512

289611BV00002B/21/A